CHANGING
YOUR
SIGN
CHANGING
YOUR
DESTINY
AN IMMIGRANT'S HOROSCOPE

CARMEN FIRAN

CHANGING YOUR SIGN CHANGING YOUR DESTINY

AN IMMIGRANT'S HOROSCOPE

TRANSLATION BY ALEXANDRA CARIDES

LIBRARY OF CONGRESS CATALOGING-IN-PUBLICATION DATA
Changing Your Sign, Changing Your Destiny
Authored by Carmen Firan
ISBN: 9780999461778
LCCN: 2019902181

CONTENTS

MORE ON THE ROAD 1

THE CULTURE OF IMMIGRATION 5

EMIGRANTS AND IMMIGRANTS............................. 19

FINDING YOUR HOROSCOPE 29

YEAR OF THE ...

    RAT 35

    OX 45

    TIGER.. 55

    CAT/RABBIT... 65

    DRAGON 75

    SNAKE... 85

    HORSE... 95

    SHEEP 105

    MONKEY 115

    ROOSTER... 125

    DOG 137

    PIG/BOAR 147

MORE ON THE ROAD

IF ASTROLOGY ASSUMES that fate and development of an individual depends on the position of stars and planets at the moment of birth, then, by extrapolation, we can accept that the destiny of an immigrant will also be under the influence of the position of planets, the Moon and the stars at his second birth, in a new home. The immigrant then has two destinies: one by birth, in his native home and another one by his second birth, in his adopted country.

This Horoscope of the Immigrant evolved from numerous observations and interactions with immigrants from diverse cultures, from careful research of the two zodiacs, Western and Asian, intertwining their differences, likeliness and compatibilities. It is, in the end, an intuitive read, somewhat speculative and playful depicting the psychology of the immigrant torn between his two births, the biological one in his native home and the symbolical one in his adopted land. Any immigrant will admit that each time he meets new people, he is asked: "What year did you come here?"

In New York, where I've been living for more than 20 years, everyone seems to have come from somewhere else. We are a cocktail of races, cultures and ethnicities. While there are some common features to all immigrants, like the ability to adapt to a new place, as well as identity crises, there are also individual traits, connected to the moment and motivation of our emigration, be it for political or economic reasons. At a closer look, there are similarities between immigrants who leave during a certain historic event, like economic recession or war. For instance, émigrés from Eastern Europe who left their homes before the fall of Communism were driven to emigration by different reasons than the ones who left their countries after 1989, when Communism in the Western world collapsed.

The book will interest anyone, immigrant or not, temporarily uprooted or forever moved to a foreign locale, even one toying with the idea of emigration. The reader, willing to play along, can unravel certain similarities, truths or surprising coincidences that apply to himself and his existential adventure.

In the end, we are all potential emigrants. Who can say honestly that he has never dreamt of making a change, starting fresh somewhere else? Some never leave out of fear, others out of inertia; some are sentimental, others have conviction. But however content and happy one can be in his native home, who can say, truthfully, that he never thought of how life could have been had he been born somewhere else?

I often hear "If I only had the strength to leave…" or "Had I been wise enough to stay…" There are no perfect worlds, nor ideal countries. Emigration sometimes is only an idea crossing our minds, offering an 'out', a solution to an impossible situation, when the windows and doors around us slam shut and we find ourselves with no escape in sight. The idea of emigration gives people hope; theoretically they can always try something else, somewhere else. You need to have a dream, not necessarily see it come true. By the same token, you don't need to leave a place, just know you can. At the end of the day, it is all about the Journey.

THE CULTURE OF IMMIGRATION

MOST IMMIGRANTS claim that once uprooted from their birth place, they are born again in their adopted country, into another culture with different traditions and values. Even the stars above their heads shine differently. Is it possible that through this transmutation the immigrant receives a new destiny, generated by his second birth? The horizon he faces is new, he will have new ambitions and opportunities; he will have different hopes and anxieties never encountered in his previous life. He will be thrown into deep waters and forced to learn how to swim on his own, confronting currents and storms in an unknown environment for which he has not yet developed skills or a defense mechanism.

Emigration is a culture of uprooting, with all its consequences: anxieties, uncertainties, sometime anger and hostility, other times bravado and the suppression of memories. Often immigrants have a fear of not being accepted, of not succeeding as expected—especially in the eyes of those left behind—they dread disappointment and feel guilty for having left their motherland and are also afraid to fail in their adopted country.

At the same time, this culture of emigration assumes changes in the immigrant's mentality, the development of new traits, specific to the change of destiny, the push to smother and forget negative habits and develop other ones, useful in his new adventure: courage, decisiveness, determination, ambition, sacrifice. Sometimes, this process may also bring along additional psychological issues: alienation, opportunism, social climbing, greed, selfishness, envy of the native jealousy towards other immigrants who made it there quicker or easier.

The word *foreigner* has profound meanings and complex connotations in all languages. The word *stranger* has a similar meaning in English, derived from *strange*, also a synonym with *odd*. In America, an official term for someone born outside the country is *alien*, (synonymous with *extra-terrestrial*). An immigrant is the "extra-terrestrial" who chooses a new place to land. He reinvents himself on the go. He is the *odd-stranger* born out of himself at some point in his life. The immigrant, an alien who oscillates between reshaping his identity and rebuilding his ethnic nest, tries to adapt while saving his traditions and cultural heritage. This Horoscope addresses the split destiny of the immigrant—being born twice in one single life.

EMIGRATION IS LIKE A DIVORCE. The emigrant doesn't only divorce his motherland, his home and language, but also the air and water he grew up in, his ancestral environment. He leaves his biological mother and has to get under the skin of a step-mother, gain her trust and develop a relationship which should allow him to grow and manifest himself beyond her suspicions and resentments.

Some immigrants take their home along with them, others cut themselves open, forcing the process of healing through adjustment. While some dream to be assimilated as soon as possible and want to be treated as 'equals' at the cost of losing their identity, others are opposed to being assimilated in any form and want to be accepted just as they are.

There are those who keep living in their motherland, virtually. Others amputate their home from their sentimental memory, willingly. Some don't know where their home is anymore. Others carry two homes around, accepting their duplicitous identity—these are the happy immigrants, they have made peace with the past and found their balance in the present, wherever they may be.

AN IMMIGRANT CARRIES IT ALL with him while, at the same time, letting go of many possessions and beliefs. With time, he will sift through his stuffed luggage and fill in the holes in his emotional dowry. He will find that many of the values he considered indispensable when he left and which he tried hard to save and bring over with him, have become obsolete or useless. Other ideas and values will enter his life to bring him the certainty and stability he needs.

The day he feels self-assured and relaxed, when he reaches a certain level of material comfort and clarifies for himself the emotional baggage which followed his uprooting, is the day the immigrant is able to look back to his motherland and understand and accept all his unresolved memories, guilt, regrets and debts—real or imaginary.

Theoretically, everyone leaves their home country for a better life. But any dramatic change of fate, like emigration, is a risky and courageous enterprise, with no guarantee of success. It only presents different possibilities. Once the Pandora's box is opened, unpredictable forces and equally random challenges come out, forcing the emigrant to take on a new set of characteristics, ranging from finding the strength to make it through unexpected difficulties to having the flexibility for adaptation. The immigrant must find himself a place inside the mechanism governing his new life. He needs to use his talent to penetrate the new world so that he is able to, ultimately, shoot for the stars.

Once his artificial and forced re-implantation happens in foreign soil, the immigrant is, de facto, changing his micro-cosmos. The air and water have a different consistency from those he was born and raised with. The cuisine is different, and his body needs some time to get used to another style; his metabolism must adjust his biological and emotional levels. Some put on weight (especially in America), others become thinner or discover reactions borrowed from the specifics of the new place (from neuroses to allergies). A Chinese immigrant once told me that he only started having trouble with allergies when he immigrated to America eight years before. I joked, replying that it meant he'd adapted. He ignored my humor and said that this was his body signaling his incompatibility with the new environment for which he had no defense mechanism.

ADAPTATION IS THE KEY, even obsessive, challenge for an immigrant.

Duplicitous as he is, the immigrant will use even more duplicitous methods when embracing a new value system. He will sometimes pretend to like things he actually detests, only to prove to himself that he is *adapting*. Other times he will stubbornly go against the wave, proclaiming his adaption in his own terms.

A French professor at Colombia University who immigrated to America years ago said that being an intellectual immigrant in New York is a privilege worth being cherished and preserved. He will always be perceived as a precious addition to the native family of thinkers or artists, coming with a fresh perspective, with originality, enriching ideas and skills.

The president of a design company in New York once told me that she prefers to hire young European immigrants for their creativity and artistic sense. Other companies appreciate the hard-working trait of Asian employees, while yet others prefer to hire Latin-American workers who they believe are modest and lack pretense.

In New York, the services provided by immigrants are generally somehow separated by culture and nationality: the beauty salons have French or Russian owners, Koreans are generally proprietors of *delis*, laundromats are managed by Chinese, jewelry stores are Israeli-owned. Most buildings are maintained by Albanians, while limo companies are usually owned by Hispanics, many accounting offices belong to Greeks, gardening is a Latin-American business, one finds Pakistanis and Mexicans in the construction business and so on ... and in spite of all these traditional stereotypes, everything is fluid, in continuous change.

A few decades ago, for example, southern Manhattan's Lower East Side was densely populated by Jews—it's now become Chinatown, which also has extended over the neighboring Little Italy; old American families who lived in Forest Hills chose to move toward Long Island, while little by little, wealthy Chinese immigrants from Hong Kong moved in. Traditionally, religious Jews immigrated to Brooklyn, while Bukharin Jews, who immigrated from the ex-Soviet Republics, have grown roots in Rego Park. Queens might be the largest ethnic Babylon, each of its neighborhoods being dominated by a community of immigrants: Greeks and East-Europeans in Astoria, Chinese in Flushing,

Indians and Hispanics in Jackson Heights, Pakistanis and Afghans in Ozone Park, Cubans in Corona, Romanians in Ridgewood, Russians in Rego Park.

Each of these immigrants, born under their own zodiac, will be under the influence of a community horoscope in which differences will somewhat fade away in light of the dominance of the place, while their common astrological characteristic will originate from the period they chose to leave their motherland. For immigrants from Eastern Europe, the year 1989, which brought the fall of Communism, is an important milestone. The immigrants before 1989 have a different fate from the ones who immigrated after that time.

According to the Asian zodiac, 1989 is the year of the Horse, described as a period of confrontation and big challenges, with possible social turmoil that can trigger waves of emigrants following dramatic changes in their countries.

During Eastern European Communism, when the borders were closed and deprivation of liberty reached outrageous peaks, emigration was a very courageous act. Illegal border crossing could result in jail, torture, even death. A friend from New York, an immigrant from Eastern Europe, once told me how he couldn't travel back home for his mother's funeral because he didn't yet have a green card. Others were declared deserters by the Communist regimes they had escaped from, and were forbidden to return home. The emigrant before 1989 knew that with his departure he was closing a heavy iron door behind him, one that could remain forever sealed. Emigration was a traumatic and desperate act which might leave profound psychological scars.

The year 1989 opens that door, slammed with anger or despair upon the emigrants' departure, daring their fate once more. Freed from the constraints brought on by Communist dictatorships, the countries also change. New opportunities and financial prospects arise; some emigrants—well-established by now somewhere else—may consider investing in their motherland's economy or getting involved in the development of new democratic structures. Some others may look into taking back their abandoned or confiscated real estate hoping to spend their golden years in their homeland. And, why not, once close to retirement, with little or no family left, they may even contemplate returning for good to their native land...

The unexpected turn of events ignited by the fall of Communism could affect and emotionally destabilize immigrants who haven't quite made their home in their adopted country. When Communism in Europe vanished, it took with it the main motivation for emigration—to be in a free country. Frustration or strong egos may prevent some immigrants from facing-up to their failure in their adopted land. Admitting their struggles with financial or economic difficulties could be especially hard if family and friends in their native country became successful, professionally or financially.

THE IMMIGRANT COUPLE is also vulnerable to transformations and challenges which might not have occurred in their native land. I know couples who went through important changes after immigration. For some, being far away from their country of birth and facing new obstacles brings them closer together and they pull at the same cart for the prosperity of their family. Nevertheless, many couples lose their balance. Uprooting each partner from his/her native land to the adoptive country represents a double divorce for the couple. Each one reacts in his or her own way, and is able—or not—to find the resources to survive. Some close-up ranks around their children. Others don't find, even in their offspring, a good enough reason to continue their lives together.

I met a couple of artists who emigrated from Eastern Europe after the fall of Communism. Each one had to redefine himself in America: she left her acting career to become a kindergarten teacher in Queens, while he, once an acclaimed musician, became a computer specialist in Brooklyn. They went on to have two children, bought a car and a condominium and spent a few vacations back in their native country, now going through an economic expansion. That's when frustrations started. The ex-actress started to gain weight, and the ex-musician spent more and more time sitting in front of his computer. Dissatisfaction and stress crept up and affected their sex life. She started to talk about returning home to her mother, while he didn't want to. Some of his old friends in his native country were quite successful after the fall of Communism, became IT specialists, were well paid and owned expensive cars and vacation homes—all the more reason to avoid encountering them.

The pressure to make more and more money as quickly as possible is another source of stress for some immigrant couples. They split-up only when they have achieved a higher standard of living. The wife of a friend of mine who emigrated from Central America, once told me: 'We stayed together and we are doing well. God kept us out of trouble: we didn't win the lottery...'

Sometimes, between a couple, a new competitive feature arises: competition with one another. The more successful partner takes control and blames the other for his incapacity at keeping up. On the other hand, the less fortunate partner could become inhibited and vulnerable, nursing a guilt likely to turn into psychosis, or ignite a dramatic, troubled personality change.

Men are most vulnerable in immigrant couples. Their psychology gravitates more around their ego, self-esteem, self-assurance, the need to prove themselves, to be respected for their performance. Men need the admiration of women they are close to. Couples who emigrated from *macho* cultures like those in South America or Eastern Europe, are shocked to find their traditions contradicted by American society, with feminism balancing the powers between genders, sometimes even overturning it... American women consider their careers, professional and financial achievements, as *the* priority, followed by family or relationships. Thus, they may end up surpassing their partner, financially and also emotionally. All of which can also happen within the dynamics of immigrant couples.

A Russian artist I know, renowned in his country, immigrated to America when he was about 43 years old. His wife, a high-school design teacher in Moscow, was a bit younger. Five years later, the painter had still not found his place in the artistic world of Los Angeles. He painted sporadically and his works were not selling. Fate smiled upon his wife though: she was in the right place at the right time and rose from a cosmetologist employed in a Beverly Hills beauty salon, to partner of the same salon, owned by another Russian woman who had immigrated at the beginning of the '70s. While the wife now has a glamorous life, the painter feels humiliated by his failure and his wife's successes. He became profoundly depressed, secluded, dependent on alcohol and anti-depressants, and, sadly, it all ended on his 50st-birthday with his suicide.

In couples with partners who immigrated from different cultures, there is a risk of dysfunction stemming from an inability to communicate. An Italian writer separated from her English husband five years after immigrating to America. She told me how their differences in temperament, in dealing with life issues in general, became insurmountable once on neutral foreign land.

It is interesting to note that couples who immigrated from Eastern Europe before 1989 are more stable and secure than those who immigrated after the year Communism fell. Perhaps the common enemy in their native country—dictatorship, with all its fears and uncertainties—acted as a link at a subconscious level, to keep them together even after their escape to foreign soil?

From inside the immigrant enclaves, the new arrivals are perceived as lucky. Whether they fled for political or economic reasons, friends back home admire their courage to start from scratch, or envy them for their success in their new home.

THE MOST SENSITIVE ELEMENT for an emigrant is, after all, the mother tongue. It is an expression of the identity and heritage of the emigrant and represents the strongest connection with their native home. Unaffected by distance and time, by concessions and surrenders, by compromises, failures and achievements, the mother tongue always provides the certainty of a refuge, a spiritual shelter, a cultural intimacy with their native land.

The mother tongue is the language of dreams, the language the immigrant talks to himself in and the language of his subconscious, even after he immigrates to another culture, sometime up until the end of his life. I know immigrants who say that they have never dreamt of themselves anywhere else other than in their native land; all their dreams are about the country they left. Some even stopped dreaming for a while.

A foreign language unused for a long time is lost, while the mother tongue, even unspoken for decades, remains hidden in the immigrant's spiritual dowry, loyal, mysterious, holding together the essence of the ancestral universe, the particularities and the spirit of their native land.

AMERICA IS THE BEST EXAMPLE of an amalgam of immigrant cultures, some strengthened through generations, others still new. It is also the place where this amalgam is coherent—all the immigration dramas from yesterday or today, considered. Today however, the official attitude is one hostile to immigration: restricting citizenship for permanent residence on welfare programs, canceling the visa lottery, and limiting integration of families split between America and other countries. Isolationist tendencies have consequences in the long run, not only inside America, but also for the perception of the country abroad.

THE IMMIGRANT IS A TREE with amputated roots. A floating tree, rooted in the air rather than in the ground, whose roots can regrow in a different place, or remain hanging forever. Understanding his destiny is the immigrant's best shield from the storms to come.

EMIGRANTS AND IMMIGRANTS

THE DESIRE TO FIND OUT what the future has in store for us seems as absurd as normal—a pursuit dating back to times immemorial. The relationship between the skies, Earth and the human being was explored by the oldest civilizations. The Mayan solar calendars, astral maps and stone sundials, the Egyptian pyramids, zodiacs and future-seers place death and birth in close connection with cosmic entities trying to explain the limits of life, foretell the future and make sense of it all. Science, and religion separate in their quests only to reach the same dilemmas and fears: fear of future, of time, of death …

Astrology connects the macro- and micro-cosmos, reflecting upon the dependency of personal destiny of an individual with the configuration of the planets and the position of the stars at birth. Fundamentally, the interdependence between Earth's elements represents a concerted demonstration of the coherence of the universe. Egyptians, for instance, believed the configuration of stars at birth to be of extreme importance, predicting individual destinies.

History shows that scores of kings and heads of state kept an astrologist nearby, available to consult not only on telling their futures or possible natural disasters, but also on political decisions. To this day, the Indian parliament reserves a seat for an astrologist. In many Asian countries and cultures, an astrologist thoroughly analyzes the horoscopes of romantic partners to determine compatibility, and, only afterwards, approves their matrimony. It is well-known that Nancy Reagan, President Ronald Reagan's wife, used to confer with an astrologist when her husband had important decisions to make.

The fascination of 'reading the stars' is still alive today; horoscopes are delivered electronically in the modern world through the Internet.

Western and Eastern astrology are different, although both are based on birth dates and use symbols to illustrate their theories. The Chinese horoscope assumes that people born in the same year will share similar existential experiences; the Western zodiac considers the day and month of birth to define one's destiny. The differences reflect the fact that Eastern civilizations value generational differences, while Western cultures focus more on individual psychological aspects.

THE **WESTERN CALENDAR** is determined by the movement of the Earth around the Sun, marking the beginning of a month on a given date and the month's end 28–31 days later. The Western zodiac is based on the position of constellations in the sky over the 12 months of the year. Therefore, January is associated with Capricorn because this constellation is at its zenith during this month, while July is connected with the sign of Cancer because the constellation Cancer is most visible then.

The four elements (**Water, Fire, Earth** and **Air**) essentially define one's psychology and temperament at birth. The personality of the emigrants can also be characterized by the common features of these signs:

The Emigrant of **Water** (**Cancer**, **Scorpio** or **Pisces**) is flexible, easy-going, takes the shape of the space he occupies; he handles himself well against insurmountable odds. Sometimes an idealist, or a dreamer, he meanders through difficult times and ends up following his own way.

The Emigrant of **Fire** (**Aries**, **Leo** or **Sagittarius**) is a fighter, capable of big sacrifices, while also taking on big risks. Motivated by his ambition to "make it", he is a determined conqueror of his adopted land at the price of burning his roots and being born again from his own ashes.

The Emigrant of **Earth** (**Taurus**, **Virgo** or **Capri-corn**) needs safety and stability, a solid footing in his new land, is a practical person, functional and clear. Nevertheless, he is nostalgic for his homeland, attached to its traditions, a conservative soul who transplants his kitchen, music and habits, good or bad, into exile with him.

The Emigrant of **Air** (**Gemini**, **Libra** or **Aquarius**), a tree with his roots in the air, is always ready to return home if favorable, or beneficial changes happened back there. However, he can also immigrate multiple times to different places. Forever wandering, this emigrant is like a migrating bird, drawn to warmer places; he floats around forever, building temporary nests here and there. His destiny is the road, the flight. He is the wanderer who swings over worlds he contemplates without breaking away for good or settling anywhere.

THE MOON, by its proximity to Earth, exercises its influence on water bodies. Flux and reflux of the seas and oceans depend on the Moon's magnetic attraction. The Moon is essential in the Chinese culture, establishing the correlation between destiny and cosmos, starting from the premise that three quarters of the human body is water.

The structure of the **CHINESE CALENDAR** is based on the phases of the moon, considered essential in determining one's temperament at birth. For instance, born under a new moon are the adventurers, courageous, creative people, while prudent and diplomatic natures are born under the full moon.

In a 28-day cycle, the Moon completes its trajectory between the Sun and the Earth. It appears larger and larger during the first 14 days, up to a Full Moon, then diminishes for the next 14 days, down to a New Moon. The first 14 days of the Lunar cycle are considered favorable to new endeavors, a time which stimulates creativity. It is an optimal time to initiate important activities with a high degree of difficulty. The old saying '*do the right thing at the right time,*' is attributed to this period. According to ancient beliefs, it is unfavorable to start any endeavors and new beginnings on the 14th day of the cycle, when the Moon is waning. During this stretch of 14 days, it is best to only continue ongoing activity, avoid confrontations and mistakes.

The Chinese Zodiac, dating back to the first Chinese Emperor, approx. 2636 B.C., is made up of long cycles of 60 years, each cycle subdivided into simple sets of 12 years. To each year, an animal is attributed, *the animal hidden in our heart.* According to legend, before leaving this world, Buddha summoned all the animals to bid them good-bye. Only twelve animals showed up, and Buddha rewarded them by naming a Chinese year after each of them, in the order they answered his call: The Rat, The Ox, The Tiger, The Cat, The Dragon, The Snake, The Horse, The Sheep, The Monkey, The Rooster, The Dog and The Pig.

The first to arrive was the Rat because he moved strategically and was able to sneak through anything to quickly reach his target. The last one was the Pig, meticulous and prudent. The Chinese tradition holds true that the animal governing the year a person is born in, greatly influences his personality. Similarly, the animal governing the birth of the immigrant in the new land affects his temperament and the actions the immigrant takes as he adapts to the new environment.

Because the Chinese calendar is based on the 28-day Moon cycles, the beginning of each year falls during an interval between January 1st and mid-February, rather than on a given day. For example, The Year of The Rat starts on February 7th 2008 and ends on January 25th 2009, The Year of The Horse starts on January 27th 1990 and ends on February 14th 1991, and so on.

During the 60-year cycle, each year of the twelve zodiac animals combines successively with the five elements defined by Chinese philosophy: **Metal** (dominated by Venus), **Water** (dominated by Mercury), **Wood** (dominated by Jupiter), **Fire** (dominated by Mars) and **Earth** (dominated by Saturn). Both the astrological sign and the element of the year influence the personality of the immigrant.

The years ending in 0 or 1 are years of **Metal**. The immigrants in these years are constant in their resolve, inflexible, resilient, even inflexible sometimes; perseverance and firmness could be called their defining traits.

The Emigrants of **Water**—the year of immigration ending in 2 and 3—are adaptable to any circumstance, flexible, intelligent and sensitive, characterized by intuition and diplomacy; they appreciate beauty and harmony.

The Emigrants of **Wood**—the year of immigration ending in 4 and 5—have integrity as their dominant trait. They are led by correctness and legality and are generous, loyal, show goodwill, although they can also by thrifty or greedy.

The Emigrants of **Fire**—the year of immigration ending in 6 or 7—are energetic, dynamic, enthusiastic, but also oscillate and could be unstable; They are always agitated and on the move. Their actions are defined by strength but also by destruction.

The Emigrants of **Earth**—the year of immigration ending in 8 or 9—are characterized by stability and conservativeness. They are traditionalists and pragmatic.

THE DESTINY OF AN IMMIGRANT could be defined by the interpretation of both dates, in a combination between the Western zodiac (at birth) and the Chinese one (for the year of immigration).

This book presents and discusses all 144 combinations between all zodiac signs.

Let's take a few examples from the horoscope of a **Capricorn** immigrant. (December 22nd–January 19th):

A **Capricorn** who immigrates in the year of the **Tiger (2010, 1998, 1986, 1974, 1962, 1950)** is fortune's favorite. An excellent fighter, while he is imaginative and resourceful, he also remains deeply rooted. With a genuine and sincere nature, he is seductive in any company and flirts fully aware of his charm. Only this second life will let him find his soul-mate, his ideal partner, as his mentality also changes. If he was self-indulgent in his native country, he now becomes unwavering and faithful. With an exceptional tamer, he will let himself be tamed.

A **Capricorn** who immigrates during the year of the **Horse (2014, 2002, 1990, 1978, 1966, 1954)** is ambitious and pragmatic and uses his intelligence to find favorable situations to profit from. He chases success and actually achieves a bit of it, but only later in life. Selfish, just like any Horse, he has trouble sharing the fruits of his labor. Few Capricorn immigrants have a wish to emigrate back to their native country. It isn't easy for them to pull away, but when they do, their departures are final. They don't hold any grudge and look back without regrets; they are generally lucky, and immigration will favor their accomplishments.

Energetic and with a tireless capacity to work, a **Capricorn** immigrant holds on to his ambition to break into high society; his successes in his adopted country are due to his unrelenting eagerness and tenacity. He is, however, less cautious and frugal than he used to be, borrowing from the generosity and liveliness of the **Dog (2018, 2006, 1994, 1982, 1970, 1958)**. Anxious and an introverted type, prudent and pessimistic—all traits of the Capricorn—are attenuated by emigration making him more dynamic, more open and confident; his second life is under the sign of sincerity, self-confidence and loyalty, all characteristics of the Dog. On one hand, life might bring difficult times upon his family, which are likely to have a deep emotional impact on him. His rewards are always his professional achievements, reaching thereby the balance he always yearned for.

The most spectacular destiny change in immigration belongs to **Capricorns** who immigrate in the year of the **Pig (2019, 2007, 1995, 1983, 1971, 1959)**. The unexpected success in his adopted country makes him generous, eager to do good deeds for both his native and adoptive lands alike. He dedicates himself to noble humanitarian pursuits, trying to reconcile his hands-on talent—which lays at the core of his wealth—with intense spiritual experiences.

FINDING YOUR HOROSCOPE

STEP 1:

Select the year of the immigration and go the chapter with the name of that animal.

See the tables below for the first and last day of a given zodiacal year:

10 FEB 1948–27 JAN 1960	
10 FEB 1948–28 JAN 1949	RAT
29 JAN 1949–16 FEB 1950	OX
17 FEB 1950–5 FEB 1951	TIGER
6 FEB 1951–26 JAN 1952	RABBIT
27 JAN 1952–13 FEB 1953	DRAGON
14 FEB 1953–2 FEB 1954	SNAKE
3 FEB 1954–23 JAN 1955	HORSE
24 JAN 1955–11 FEB 1956	GOAT
12 FEB 1956–30 JAN 1957	MONKEY
31 JAN 1957–17 FEB 1958	ROOSTER
18 FEB 1958–7 FEB 1959	DOG
8 FEB 1959–27 JAN 1960	PIG

28 JAN 1960–14 FEB 1972

28 JAN 1960–14 FEB 1961	RAT
15 FEB 1961–4 FEB 1962	OX
5 FEB 1962–24 JAN 1963	TIGER
25 JAN 1963–12 FEB 1964	RABBIT
13 FEB 1964–1 FEB 1965	DRAGON
2 FEB 1965–20 JAN 1966	SNAKE
21 JAN 1966–8 FEB 1967	HORSE
9 FEB 1967–29 JAN 1968	GOAT
30 JAN 1968–16 FEB 1969	MONKEY
17 FEB 1969–5 FEB 1970	ROOSTER
6 FEB 1970–26 JAN 1971	DOG
27 JAN 1971–14 FEB 1972	PIG

15 FEB 1972–1 FEB 1984

15 FEB 1972–2 FEB 1973	RAT
3 FEB 1973–22 JAN 1974	OX
23 JAN 1974–10 FEB 1975	TIGER
11 FEB 1975–30 JAN 1976	RABBIT
31 JAN 1976–17 FEB 1977	DRAGON
18 FEB 1977–6 FEB 1978	SNAKE
7 FEB 1978–27 JAN 1979	HORSE
28 JAN 1979–15 FEB 1980	GOAT
16 FEB 1980–4 FEB 1981	MONKEY
5 FEB 1981–24 JAN 1982	ROOSTER
25 JAN 1982–12 FEB 1983	DOG
13 FEB 1983–1 FEB 1984	PIG

2 FEB 1984–18 FEB 1996

2 FEB 1984–19 FEB 1985	RAT
20 FEB 1985–8 FEB 1986	OX
9 FEB 1986–28 JAN 1987	TIGER
29 JAN 1987–16 FEB 1988	RABBIT
17 FEB 1988–5 FEB 1989	DRAGON
6 FEB 1989–26 JAN 1990	SNAKE
27 JAN 1990–14 FEB 1991	HORSE
15 FEB 1991–3 FEB 1992	GOAT
4 FEB 1992–22 JAN 1993	MONKEY
23 JAN 1993–9 FEB 1994	ROOSTER
10 FEB 1994–30 JAN 1995	DOG
31 JAN 1995–18 FEB 1996	PIG

19 FEB 1996–6 FEB 2008

19 FEB 1996–6 FEB 1997	RAT
7 FEB 1997–27 JAN 1998	OX
28 JAN 1998–15 FEB 1999	TIGER
16 FEB 1999–4 FEB 2000	RABBIT
5 FEB 2000–23 JAN 2001	DRAGON
24 JAN 2001–11 FEB 2002	SNAKE
12 FEB 2002–31 JAN 2003	HORSE
1 FEB 2003–21 JAN 2004	GOAT
22 JAN 2004–8 FEB 2005	MONKEY
9 FEB 2005–28 JAN 2006	ROOSTER
29 JAN 2006–17 FEB 2007	DOG
18 FEB 2007–6 FEB 2008	PIG

7 FEB 2008–24 JAN 2020

7 FEB 2008–25 JAN 2009	RAT
26 JAN 2009–13 FEB 2010	OX
14 FEB 2010–2 FEB 2011	TIGER
3 FEB 2011–22 JAN 2012	RABBIT
23 JAN 2012–9 FEB 2013	DRAGON
10 FEB 2013–30 JAN 2014	SNAKE
31 JAN 2014–18 FEB 2015	HORSE
19 FEB 2015–7 FEB 2016	GOAT
8 FEB 2016–27 JAN 2017	MONKEY
28 JAN 2017–15 FEB 2018	ROOSTER
16 FEB 2018–4 FEB 2019	DOG
5 FEB 2019–24 JAN 2020	PIG

25 JAN 2020–10 FEB 2032

25 JAN 2020–11 FEB 2021	RAT
12 FEB 2021–31 JAN 2022	OX
1 FEB 2022–21 JAN 2023	TIGER
22 JAN 2023–09 FEB 2024	RABBIT
10 FEB 2024–28 JAN 2025	DRAGON
29 JAN 2025–16 FEB 2026	SNAKE
17 FEB 2026–5 FEB 2027	HORSE
6 FEB 2027–25 JAN 2028	GOAT
26 JAN 2028–12 FEB 2029	MONKEY
13 FEB 2029–2 FEB 2030	ROOSTER
3 FEB 2030–22 JAN 2031	DOG
23 JAN 2031–10 FEB 2032	PIG

STEP 2:

Read the chapter introduction which gives general characteristics and for a more specific reading, select your sign determined by the day and month of your birth according to the Western zodiac.

Enjoy reading the horoscope of your emigrant friends or relatives following the same steps.

MAR 21–APR 19	ARIES
APR 20–MAY 20	TAURUS
MAY 21–JUNE 20	GEMINI
JUNE 21–JULY 22	CANCER
JULY 23–AUG 23	LEO
AUG 24–SEPT 22	VIRGO
SEPT 24–OCT 22	LIBRA
OCT 23–NOV 21	SCORPIO
NOV 22–DEC 20	SAGITTARIUS
DEC 22–JAN 19	CAPRICORN
JAN 20–FEB 18	AQUARIUS
FEB 19–MAR 20	PISCES

YEAR OF THE
RAT

Immigrants who arrived in their new country in the Year of the **Rat** are prudent people, even sparing when it comes to their wealth, for fear of going back to the Poor House and reliving their birth-destiny. At the same time, they wish to protect their assets and save up as insurance against hard times, or, simply, a future in which they see themselves working less and enjoying life more. They have a sense of danger and know how to detect traps.

Immigration stimulates their creativity and imagination; they are resourceful but avoid hard labor or extended hours of work. Nevertheless, they have their own winning strategy. Quick and nimble, **Rat** immigrants have a knack for finding their *right way*, circumventing dangerous situations and choosing the shortest and best route. Sometimes they find their *best* way in life, but only in their later years.

Born contemplative, nostalgic and earth-bound, immigrants in this group have trouble adapting to the new world they have landed in, as they hold on to old memories.

Without many adventurous streaks, the immigrants in the Year of the **Rat**, are energetic and passionate, with intense feelings and strong instincts, with a well-developed, sophisticated, sensory inner world, which allows them to easily detect emotional and physical signals. They also have a fine sense of humor.

An **Aries (March 21–April 19)** who immigrated in the year of the Rat displays an exuberant, impetuous personality whenever he wants to impress. He plans his attack and retreat equally well; in a flash he goes from harsh to moody. Nevertheless, this immigrant expects to be spoiled and listened to by his family and friends. He pretends to be interested in people or situations and even spends time and energy to maintain relationships but only if he perceives a potential gain. Being in control of a situation brings out his generosity in love and business. He will fight for success in his new life, but will slow down after a while and look for profitable situations to secure a comfortable future for himself.

A **Taurus (April 20–May 20)** is enslaved to his conveniences and habits. Conventional, conservative, with rigid views, hard-working but stubborn and often lacking a sense of humor, he is a steady partner in the long run, a dedicated parent and an honorable citizen in society. However, if something doesn't go his way, he may very well display a lack of good manners. His achievements are more significant in his adopted land than they would have been had he stayed home. He is profoundly sensual, a weakness which could make him vulnerable to sentimental traps. When in love, his world turns upside-down: he is willing to do anything, take any risk to maintain his love affair.

The **Gemini (May 21–June 20)** immigrant is a social butterfly. He loves beauty and elegance above all and easily adapts to any situation. Emigration appeals to him only if it proves to be easy and comes with a guaranteed win. Most of the time, he sees his dream come true, either by pure luck, or the support of people around him who've been seduced by his charm. However, you cannot truly rely on him. He lets you down when you need him most; he's unpredictable, with his head in the clouds, eternally attracted by yet another scent and nuance. He spreads himself too thin. Nonetheless, he can be a Renaissance Man, passionate about the arts or with a highly spiritual education.

Writer Joseph Brodsky and actress Natalie Portman are in this group.

A **Cancer (June 21–July 22)** native who immigrated in the Year of the Rat cares a lot about aesthetics, is sensitive and drawn to poetry and romanticism. His strength is having a personal approach. He can convince his partner of just about anything, receiving favors and rewards in return. A Cancer's ability to use his physical qualities to impress and conquer, combined with the sentimentalism of the Rat, are the aces up his sleeve which will help the immigrant in this group succeed through marriage or partnership. He is curious inventive; he likes to break the rules and go against the wave.

Nikola Tesla is an example.

The **Leo (July 23–August 23)** doesn't shoot from behind or take useless victims. Never content with his achievements, he always wants more and never accepts defeats or failures. Luckily he doesn't often lose, being a winner by definition. After a rocky start, immigration will propel him up in the social world and will bring him numerous professional achievements. He will stay active until late in life and won't get sour with age. He will keep up a merciless sense of humor and fresh irony, which, in turn, will always make him desired company, delighting any audience with his wit and charm.

People born under the sign of **Virgo (August 24–Sept 22)** and who immigrated during the Year of the Rat, will continue their destiny without many changes.

Perhaps that is due to the similarity in personality and character between the two signs of the Western and Asian zodiacs? These people are born collectors and antiquarians, pedant and organized. Loyal to their friends and family, they are willing to compromise to save a relationship. While pleasant and elegant in society, their sharp criticism is always present. Their reactions and bitter comments can sometimes be surprising, uttered with a subtle arrogance, hidden under a soft, gentle façade. They are courageous and risk takers.

Anousheh Ansari, Iranian engineer and space tourist, is among them.

If you are born a **Libra (Sep 23–Oct 22)**, immigration during the Year of the Rat, brings you more patience and wisdom, prudence, and tenacity to wait for the favorable moment to make it big in your new country, both professionally and on a personal level. This immigrant is thrifty though doesn't short change himself in anyway. His enthusiasm and joie-de-vivre energize his entourage and stimulate people to engage in courageous projects or to attempt daring professional and intellectual challenges. Although a good listener, adviser and mediator, he does come across as too intransigent at times, based on his strong beliefs. If he ever happens to cross his own lines, he does it very carefully, protecting his public image at all cost.

The **Scorpio native (Oct 23–Nov 21)** is a perfect public speaker, educated and disciplined, with an acute sense of critique, who enjoys good conversation—at times a bit gossipy. His sharp *bites* and irony, humorous nevertheless, can be uncontrollable. He isn't too creative, but he could excel either in research—being the academic and authoritative type—or as a good, honorable professional. He succeeds in his new country, but has trouble making friends and prefers to live in his own mysterious emotional retreat.

A **Sagittarius (Nov 22–Dec 21)** is as much cerebral as he is intuitive, has sound instincts and knows when destiny half-opens a door. Then he knows when to put his foot in that door and push, driven by his fighter nature more than just ambition, often helped by luck rather than persistence. He is an elegant, distinguished person, drawn toward the arts and nature, appreciates beauty and harmony in life. A Sagittarius despises mediocrity and becomes quite 'the cynic' in a society below his intellectual level. Born under a Fire sign, after immigration he behaves like a mixture of Water and Air-signs—flexible and adaptable. He carries his home around on his back and is able to make up his bed on the seashore, at the foot of a mountain or in the middle of a crowded street.

Andrew Carnegie is part of this group.

Emigration worsens personality defects for a **Capricorn (Dec 22–Jan 19)** and changes his temperament. Taking in a self-preservation mechanism from the adoptive culture, he adheres to those spiritual movements which satisfy his ego to stay forever young and delay death. He manages to delude himself with promises of success and happiness, only to end up cutting off his old solid ties and sacrificing sentimental relationships. To reach his goals, he may even turn into a true manipulator, juggling people and situations and pushing many legal limits in the process. Cunning and calculated, he manages to always land on his feet. Only later on will he sense the injuries he's inflicted on others, by then finding himself alone with his sand-castles collapsing one by one.

An **Aquarius (Jan 20–Feb 18)** faces a rough start in immigration, with various frustrations. He will become accomplished late in life, as he reaches a reconciliation with himself, more so than in his youth, although he won't be as happy. A Good Samaritan, he spends his energy helping others. He is exceptionally good at carrying out tasks. Docile and patient, he can change the face of the Earth, or get demoralized if unappreciated. He is never bored and is very rich spiritually, always interested in the new and original, whether he finds it in a book or in life experiences.

The **Pisces (Feb 19–Mar 20)** who immigrated in the Year of the Rat holds on to old memories. He collects antiques and rare treasures. Silently carrying around his regrets, he puts up a serene face. He dreams of a large family, in the hope of reaching stability and certainty in life. Nonetheless, he is unstable emotionally, with contradictory manifestations oscillating between goodness-of-heart and harshness, enthusiasm and depression. He swims against the current, putting himself in danger of either falling or being stranded on an unwelcoming shore.

YEAR OF THE
OX

Immigrants in the year of the **Ox** are people who fulfill their duty at all cost and by any means. Their mind is well organized and performs best if clearly motivated by objectives and rewards. Strong ties to the material world make these immigrants choose work that guarantees a high standard of living.

Ox build their relationships based on interests rather than connections. They are stubborn, cling to ideas and follow up on decisions blindly, sometimes to their own detriment. Conceited, they hide their profound dislike for arguments or offenses by staying calm, but inside they are boiling. In fact, they always wear a mask of sorts, to suit the moment. They strive to project a brilliant, spectacular social image, and can make good leaders.

Immigrants in the year of the **Ox** are eager to find earthly, practical stability. They are honest, reliable and trustworthy.

Disappointments in love could drive the **Ox** to find refuge in work, shutting himself off from the rest of the world.

The **Aries (Mar 21–Apr 19)** immigrating under the sign of the Ox are courageous, ready to take great risks to change their destiny. Whether they are adventurous, attracted to the unknown, or escapees from a totalitarian regime, the emigrants of this astral combination push their luck and borders alike, and are determined to make it on their own. They will take the bull by the horn facing new challenges in their adopted country, and will end up with a new, softer and less aggressive personality, all the while remaining stubborn and ambitious.

Practical, realistic and hard-working, a **Taurus (April 20–May 20)** holds on to his dreams and gives up only if his feelings are hurt. Emigration is an unattractive proposition to him. He hates change and needs stability. Unwavering and conservative by nature, he is loyal to his habits, friends and family. A tough exterior hides a sentimental nature. Immigration during the year of the Ox is good for him, as this sign is closest to his own. His organized mind will be an asset in his adopted country, helping him build a safe and bright future.

Writer Vladimir Nabokov is among them.

A **Gemini** (May 21–June 20) immigrating during the year of the Ox is duplicitous, like a Pisces, as indecisive as a Libra, adaptable and in continuous motion like an Aquarius, spontaneous, inventive and adventurous like an Aries, and as curious and gossip-loving as a Virgo. The sign of the Ox, which defines his new destiny, magnifies his nervous and ambivalent personality. He is the eternal émigré, possessing many destinies inside himself: tenacious—like a Snake, kind—resembling a Goat, pleasant—similar to a Horse, Monkey-like opportunistic and Cat-like intuitive. A surprise is always in store for him!

A **Cancer** (June 21–July 22) needs clear, precise goals and guaranteed rewards to convince him to emigrate. Even with all the preparation, he carefully plans that moment to avoid frustrations or hardships in his adopted country. He knows how to pick the right moment to succeed, without inconveniencing himself. He is also a master of manipulation, uses compassionate people who naively believe in his legendary, sensitive nature. If, however, his direct interests are under attack, his cruel, unpleasant side quickly surfaces. A grateful receiver, he gives back very little. In the end, this Ox-Cancer immigrant is prudent, and his lucky stars shine above him.

A **Leo** (**July 23–Aug 23**) who immigrates during the year of the Ox will never be at peace. He may change continents, emigrate multiple times if need be, until he finds and defines the territory he can control, regardless of the cost. Dominant, devouring and possessive, a Leo needs to be the leader anywhere: whether he is in charge of large crowds or a tiny fishing boat. He is a know-it-all who always needs to have the last word. If you do not keep up with him, you are crushed without mercy. He can make the ultimate sacrifice for his loved ones, but can also sacrifice everything to satisfy his ego which demands superiority while reigning over bowed heads. The year of the Ox bestows emotional instability upon him, with rage and stubborn outbursts. Although life could give him all, that promise doesn't necessarily make him happy. He will, nevertheless, put up a glorious face, complete with a frozen smile.

Virgos (**Aug 24–Sept 22**) carry their routines and phobias wherever immigration takes them. The year of the Ox strengthens their practical side and need for organization, to the point of making it all look dull and boring to an outsider. Meticulous and pedantic, they recreate their native customs and rituals in immigration. Returning to the motherland is a possibility, if the changes needed to remain in their adopted country are too big, and daily life requires them to abandon routines, their energy source. A sharp critical sense and a need for perfection makes Virgo immigrants eternally disgruntled people, wherever their home may be. They find refuge in work, but only if it pleases them and doesn't require major effort.

The **Libra (Sept 23–Oct 22)** is a splendid mediator, a born negotiator, tolerant, and eager to surround himself with harmony and understanding. He decides to emigrate only after deep consideration and analysis of the risks. The reason lies in his desire to hold on to the lively social life and prestige he'd worked hard to achieve in his native country. Indecisive but enthusiastic, the sign of the Ox suits him perfectly. He doesn't shy away from hard work. A good fight is stimulating, and the stars are lined up for him. He becomes popular in his adopted country as well. His positive attitude and professional qualities make him attractive to friends all around.

A **Scorpio (Oct 23–Nov 21)** immigrated during the year of the Ox gladly accepts a challenge and doesn't shy away from inciting one in return. Not necessarily lucky in love, he might marry a few times. The choice of a partner in his adopted country could be dictated by common interests rather than love. On the other hand, he excels professionally. Somewhat shy, he doesn't show his feelings or his true colors, all along holding a trump card up his sleeve. When it comes to people he could use to his advantage, he is a generous opportunist, a seducer by conversation, albeit sometimes deceitful. The adopted country brings him professional success, much more than he experienced in his native land, but at the cost of becoming emotionally unstable and vulnerable.

A **Sagittarius (Nov 22–Dec 21)** immigrating during the year of the Ox has the makings of a champion. Nevertheless, and even though all stars shine upon him, he might still come up empty-handed at the other end. He does, however, put on a brave face, changing reality and pretending to be a winner in his imaginary realm. Among friends, he shines, optimistic and positive, has a gift of make-believe, but solitude finds him rather melancholic. In his adopted country he bravely faces difficulties, but could be demoralized if he sees no light at the end of the tunnel.

A **Capricorn (Dec 22–Jan 19)** could not choose better timing for his immigration than the year of the Ox. Ambitious, stubborn and courageous, he is ready to start over, successfully reinventing himself socially, professionally or personally. And what a winner he will be, even emigrating to Mars! Nothing is too difficult for him. He is ready to risk anything for his goals. A fatalist by nature, he envisions the worst scenario and continuously lives under a perceived threat, but it all fuels his real or imaginary daily battles.

The year of the Ox brings big changes to the personality of an **Aquarius (Jan 20—Feb 18)** immigrant. Generous, altruistic, social, and loquacious, an Aquarius adapts easily to his new world, guided by strong instincts. He is intuitive and malleable. He likes being in someone's shadow, preferably a strong person whom he can support as an excellent adviser and doer. The year of the Ox makes immigration easy for him, providing resources for greater personal accomplishment. Although secretly wishing more for himself, he settles for anything provided his loved ones are happy and content. A more complex personality than meets the eye, he is intense and has a rich personal world compensating for a routine life as an immigrant or the vagaries of family relationships.

The duality of a **Pisces (Feb 19–Mar 20)**, enhanced by an émigré's destiny, is best illustrated in the year of the Ox. There is perhaps even the same split personality of the Pisces' native. He swims at home in his adopted country, holding on to powerful fond memories of his motherland. While he couldn't stand living there anymore, he idealizes it after emigration. Born again under the sign of the Ox, a Pisces becomes materialistic. Work is his passion, his refuge when he feels undervalued or experiences emotional trauma. He pretends, puts up a brave face to impress others and enjoys praise, but he feels like a fish out of water among people who don't appreciate his qualities. He displays a calm demeanor but could burst into a rage at a moment's notice. Dominated by rigid ideas and self-consciousness, he continuously wavers between halt and attack. As a Pisces native, he is likely to be depressive. Immigration in the year of the Ox amplifies his psychological instability. While he is able to make lots of money in his adopted country, he could also easily lose it all. He is able to create, and also destroy, although he suffers remorse for the latter.

YEAR OF THE
TIGER

The **Tiger** dominates the Eastern zodiac signs with grandeur, courage, imagination, aggressiveness and energy. A fortune's favorite and a fighter, he is able to shape his destiny by making difficult and exclusive choices aiming at high spiritual and professional peaks. He will follow through with his endeavors even if it takes great personal sacrifice along the way.

Immigrants in the year of the **Tiger** can consider themselves *chosen*, although rising to the high standards imposed by this sign, which has impulsiveness as a mark, is a challenge. The winners' podium is a place where they long to be, and silently savor their triumph. Not at all fatalists, they have a dynamic role in their own destinies, pushing through any door they can stick their foot in. They can sense precisely where to look for success. If they want something, they get it by any means. They are smart and realistic, with complicated minds but straightforward in their reactions; nonetheless, they might also be interested in exploring the other side of the moon, guided by a shaman or a prophet…

The Tiger immigrants are drawn by influential people whom they seduce with their lively intelligence and from whom they seek advantages. They play their uniqueness card very skillfully and with great seductive prowess.

Emigrants in the Year of the **Tiger** live their lives on the edge and dream big.

The **Aries (Mar 21–Apr 19)** distinguishes himself through courage, spirit of adventure and inner strength, all reinforced by the sign of the Tiger. He improves his destiny through emigration. A skillful debate winner, he may however waste his energy and spread himself too thin until the next challenge, potentially falling victim to his own excesses. He fights hard to gain leadership and be listened to by the weak, although he knows close to nothing about the art of leading.

A **Taurus (Apr 20–May 20)**, who used to work for everything in life just like the Tiger, has an accelerated life rhythm in immigration. If he is lucky enough to find a partner able to stimulate him, they will build a lasting future together. However, he could also become a recluse from social life if he meets the one person who admires him for his intellectual qualities and is able to support him financially. Sensuality defines him during the first part of his life. Sentimental and possessive, he can easily become unstable if betrayed by his loved one whom he idealizes. Emigration reinforces in him the need to be in a couple, although he does not find harmony in life.

The sign of **Gemini (May 21–June 20)** is ruled by agitation. Immigrants in the year of the Tiger are more instinctive than logical. Intuitive by nature, they easily orient themselves in any labyrinth life throws them into. The Tiger's energy makes them more alert in their adoptive country. A Gemini is a born conqueror who doesn't hold on to his wins for long. And that could also be a good thing, as his choices are often imprudent and reckless.

A native **Cancer (June 21–July 22)** who immigrates during the year of the Tiger enjoys an extremely favorable change of fate: he now enters under the influence of a more powerful sign and he takes full advantage of that! The apparent incompatibility between Tiger and Cancer becomes a very successful combination in immigration. Using his sensitivity and reticence wisely, the Cancer native transforms his lamentation into an attack and seduction weapon. He carefully, intelligently, plans his rise to power and cultivates, exclusively, situations or people who serve his interests: he first softens them up only to use them later. Slowly but surely he *does* rise to the top. A Cancer who makes it to be the Tiger's equal, is not to be overlooked: he is overwhelmingly rewarded in his life in his adopted country.

Physicist and Nobel Prize winner, Enrico Fermi, is in this group.

To be born a **Leo (July 23–Aug 23)** and immigrate under the sign of the Tiger appears to be the perfect combination. However, the immigrant in this group isn't happy no matter how many assets he accumulates, or how high he rises on the professional ladder. His intense experiences, his impetuosity and the urge to exceed in everything he sets his mind on, the self-imposed stress to build and keep his empire and domination, could bring him to the brink of exhaustion and depression. Unable to savor his wins just for himself, he ends up living in continuous need for admirers and witnesses. Solitude is not his cup of tea, while crowds disappoint him. He may end up self-destructing, with all his trophies, displayed just for show.

Virgos (Aug 24–Sept 22) who immigrate during the year of the Tiger are *chosen*. They are spoiled by everyone: friends, work colleagues and life partners. They enjoy flirting, displaying a diaphanous face, all along hiding an iron fist inside a velvet glove. They are pragmatic, seemingly uninterested, and even careless. Behind this façade there is a cold, organized mind, with detailed scenarios for any undertaking. Born with a need for stability, they only find peace after succeeding in their adoptive country and securing a brilliant place at the top. A Tiger–Virgo is the perfect combination for a rich and powerful display of imagination.

Argentinian writer Jorge Luis Borges is among them.

The **Libra (Sept 23–Oct 22)** who immigrated under the sign of the Tiger is sociable, lively, chatty, and positive. In any given gathering, he can make himself likable through his tolerance and wisdom. He is, however, more suspicious than you think, needs to carefully weigh all the pros and cons before talking to someone, and even then he does not completely throw himself into one relationship or another. A lover of beauty and stability, he cares a lot about his personal comfort. Wherever emigration may take him, he builds himself a shelter, satisfying his need for balance, peace and harmony.

French-born Chinese-American cellist Yo-Yo Ma is among them.

The **Scorpio (Oct 23–Nov 21)** emigrates exactly where and when it feels just right to him. After a rough start, he succeeds in his adoptive country, obtaining a comfortable professional position. In the end, a Scorpio immigrated in the year of the Tiger is successful, in spite of anxieties and depression looming all around him, more so in the second part of his life. Charming in society, albeit not consistently, so polished and snobbish, he is less private and mysterious—although enjoying secrecy, and being less gossipy than one expects a Scorpio to be. He excels in his professional field, leaning toward research areas. His addictive personality could play tricks on him in his adopted country, pushing him to commit abuses: quite an uncommon behavior for a Tiger.

A **Sagittarius (Nov 22–Dec 21)** considers himself privileged to aim for the high peaks where the Tiger dominates. He might sometimes be superficial and that makes him succeed less than if he were able to discipline and pace himself in the process of reaching a goal. He lives to hit his targets on the bull's eye. Efficiently. Although a pragmatic hunter, he often assumes a victim's pose. In daily life he comes across as a pleasant, distinguished presence, a modern adventurer, liberal, honest and direct in conversations and reactions.

A **Capricorn** (**Dec 22–Jan 19**) who immigrates in the year of the Tiger is fortune's favorite. An excellent fighter, while he is imaginative and resourceful, he also remains deeply rooted. With a genuine and sincere nature, he is seductive in any company and flirts fully aware of his charm. Only this second life will let him find his soul-mate, his ideal partner, as his mentality also changes. If he was self-indulgent in his native country, he now becomes unwavering and faithful. With an exceptional tamer, he will let himself be tamed.

An **Aquarius** (**Jan 20–Feb 18**), with his sanguine and revolutionary temperament, is a good match for the sign of the Tiger. Nothing stays in his way of achieving a goal. Born an idealist and an optimist too, he easily puts things in perspective and copes with big challenges much better than with the small minutiae of daily life. His dreams are rather eccentric; he changes his plans as he goes along, most of the time for the better. Thriftiness is not in his nature: he makes a lot of money and loses it too easily. But he will always keep fame.

Russian dancer and choreographer Mikhail Baryshnikov is in this group.

The **Pisces** native (**Feb 19–March 20**), although slippery and duplicitous as defined by his water sign, easily adapts to the rigors of life in his adopted country. He cleverly swims with the current, lucid, modest and deliberate, and therefore would be a good match for the sign of the Tiger. This group represents the typical immigrant who comes to terms with his destiny with no resentment. The Pisces easily slip into the new routine and let themselves be swallowed by a life somewhat like the one left back home, a similarity which, in turn, comes with a safety valve.

YEAR OF THE
CAT/RABBIT

The immigrants in the year of the **Rabbit**—or the **Cat**, in some charts—have the ability to find the best way to settle into a foreign space. They have experienced no traumas because they know how to avoid risks and use diplomacy and connections with influential people who are able to ease the process of immigration for them.

Gentle, sensual and delicate, the **Cats** know how to get under anyone's skin. They use others to reach their goals. They are well-mannered and refined, leaving an impression of fragility, and proclaiming their sensitivity and need for beauty and harmony. They touch you. Elegance and freshness are their trademarks. However, the **Cats** are much stronger and tougher than what meets the eye. Also, they are as cunning as it gets. They build their public figure very carefully: impeccable, in need of admiration, caresses and praise, they want to be loved and missed by friends, as many as possible. In time, they gratify them in kind. But they don't hide their claws for anything. If criticized or found out to have duplicitous feelings, they charge and attack with no mercy, like the true felines they are. **Cats** can risk any battle, because they always land on their feet.

The immigrant in the year of the **Cat** survives any challenge, with no nostalgia for the motherland. The

Cats can be melancholic, but they are not sentimentalists; sigh only if they are abandoned, never when they leave on their own. After all, who could abandon a cat?!

The **Aries (March 21–April 19)** native who immigrates in the year of the Cat can be generous with people of interest to him, even sentimental; however, he becomes ruthless and cold if he loses interest in someone or something. Albeit stubborn, he follows his goals relentlessly. Once a goal is achieved, he basks in its glory. If this immigrant is an artist or a researcher, the change is beneficial: in the adopted country he could be prolific and inspired, could gain visibility and enjoy professional satisfaction and international recognition. An example in this group is the Czech-born writer Milan Kundera.

A **Taurus (April 20–May 20)** is well known for being able to always come out clean and find solutions to any problem. He's got perfect memory and only forgets what is convenient! His stubbornness comes in handy, helping his social climbing and self-discipline too. He can make a lot of money after immigration, thanks to his political and administrative abilities. Influenced by the sign of the Cat, he becomes more deliberate and less sentimental. He is possessive and jealous, careful with his wealth although he has bouts of generosity toward loved ones. He is like a fish in water in the new country, feeling superior to the ones left behind in his native land.

Gemini (May 21–June 20) are quite intuitive, able to seduce their audience, convince anyone of anything; they are, nevertheless, unpredictable and unstable. Light-minded, able to catch flying thoughts, they can juggle with concepts and ideas they only half-understand. Not at all the courageous type, they only like to *play the opposite*, to be the contrarian, surrounded by words of praise. Under the sign of the Cat they become professionally successful in their new country, they mature late in life, but their soul remains young, scattered to the four winds, restless and agitated. Emigration strengthens their dualism, their two-faced persona: one wise, another naïve; one serious, and another frivolous. They are capable of spectacular leaps and they can leave a mark on others.

Thomas Mann is part of this group.

A **Cancer (June 21–July 22)** native is favored by fortune under the sign of the Cat. Achieving prosperity in immigration comes from his talent to manipulate anyone who has a soft spot for him, all along giving the impression of simply deserving it all just because he exists in their life. Conceited and narcissistic, the Cancer native uses his claws just as the Cat uses hers to attack the ones who don't admire him enough or dare to criticize him. He is lazy but lucky. He avoids making any decision, dodges any responsibility, but being quite resourceful, he does, somehow, get all he wants in the end.

A **Leo** (**July 23–August 23**) is born a winner, and immigration in the year of the Cat lets him keep his podium, although less aggressively. He'd rather bask in his old glories than hunt for new ones. He is indeed the ancestral relative of the cat! Snobbish, enjoying a life of luxury and ease, he knows how to stand out. He has a sharp financial sense, is a good business man and plays by the rules, although the Cat may poke its nose into his business, tempting him to cut corners. He does always land on his feet.

A native **Virgo** (**August 24–September 22**) has an artistic nature, is sensitive, loves beauty and safety, seeks protection from a strong master whom he grows to love, but is also critical in his continuous search for perfection. He is territorial and possessive. A Cat-Virgo finds a cozy retreat where he purrs, pretending to be content with the world. It's tough to read what he's really thinking. Sometimes he gets tangled in his own plots. Latent forces are awakened in him when he emigrates, forcing him to become a pragmatic person. He faces quite a few challenges in his adoptive land. Yet through all his lamentations, more often than not, he is a winner.

Libra (Sept 23–Oct 22) natives who immigrate during the year of the Cat oscillate between will and compromise, politics and diplomacy, duty and pleasure, convenience and the urge for freedom. Having idealistic natures, they are forced to adhere to pragmatism, concealing their sensitivity under the need for control and balance. They don't believe in divinity but are afraid of it, secretly hoping to fulfill their spiritual experience late in life when social obligations will not call on them anymore. Even if they do not reach the top in their adoptive land, they always float to the surface.

A **Scorpio (Oct 23–Nov 21)** is like a quiet pond where dropping the wrong word or gesture, for example, a stone, could start a tsunami. Hidden away, with his needle concealed in a soft cushion, he springs up relentlessly if incited. An opportunistic speculator, with great accuracy he calculates the appropriate time and place, nursing just the right people useful in his social ascension. He is tenacious, hard-working and tough, and able to cope with anything. He finds refuge in research, with a real thirst for knowledge. It may also be his way to compensate for life's frustrations. Immigration during the year of the Cat brings him professional and personal achievements, but he remains uprooted.

A **Sagittarius (Nov 22–Dec 21) who** immigrated during a year of the Cat is generous, but with someone else's money. Pleasant among people who cherish him, arrogant with company he looks down on, he can either be a charming or a disturbing presence; it all depends on the chemistry of relationships involved, for which his sensors are very acute. Emigration doesn't come as a great discomfort to him, being in general mobile, flexible, a would-be adventurer, always ready for exotic trips and expeditions. Although he has a taste for luxury, he can very well adapt to a more modest standard of living.

Capricorns (Dec 22–Jan 19) who immigrated under the sign of the Cat have seven metaphorical lives, materialized in an eternal search of youth and immortality, using spiritual techniques sometimes beyond their understanding. They are devoted to the friends with whom they have a lot in common, while to those who betray them, they are ruthless and can even psychologically torment them. Their energy comes from tensions and conflicts, sometimes from their close entourage, if they sense they can be dominant. Without memories or regrets for their native land, no wish to ever visit it has room in their thinking. They live on a schedule, aiming to survive any catastrophe.

An **Aquarius (Jan 20–Feb 18)** immigrated under the year of the Cat easily gets used to any situation and condition, as difficult as it may come. He is ready to sacrifice himself for his loved ones; nonetheless, a disappointment in love makes him lose all that energy and enthusiasm and become a recluse. A good, generous person, he often finds his feelings exploited. Although he displays an indifferent face, pretending he doesn't care about anything, he does secretly hurt, being of an excessively sensitive nature. Without harboring big identity questions, a nostalgic memory of his native land stays with him throughout his life. His frame of mind doesn't really change in his adoptive country, which he looks upon as a temporary stop on a train going elsewhere. His best defense turns out to be to retreat into solitude; that is where he finds spiritual resources for survival.

An immigrant in the year of the Cat and native and native **Pisces (Feb 19–March 20)** is extravagant, sometimes snobbish, possesses a mostly genuine and creative nature and draws his strength from his ancestral home, so deeply connected to his childhood universe that his entire life is marked by it. He aspires to be free and manifests himself beyond conventions and boundaries. A visionary, independent spirit—sometimes even anarchical—an elitist, he is sophisticated and genuine. He holds on to his native country's traditions, but is unable to easily translate them in his new home. He could revolutionize any country he emigrates to.

One example is Romanian-born sculptor Constantin Brancusi.

YEAR OF THE
DRAGON

The **Dragon**—this mythic animal symbolizes indestructible force, crazy-courageous, stormy and full of explosive energies, ever pushing its limits and in the end, accomplishing what others don't even dare dream. The Dragon is the strongest sign among the Eastern zodiac. Also considered to be the luckiest, it's a symbol of ambition and stamina, of spiritual and human triumph and excellence.

All Chinese families wish to have their child born under this sign, the only one in their horoscope represented by a mythic animal. It parallels the griffin in western cultures or—in Eastern European fairy tales—and is endowed with supernatural powers, magic and magnetism. According to some ancient Asian beliefs, the years of the **Dragon** are auspicious, bringing spectacular changes at a global level.

The **Dragon** impresses by toughness and has the capacity of self-renewal following gigantic effort. At the same time, he intimidates, being perceived as a threat by weaker beings who cannot keep up with him. Nonetheless, being impatient and too self-assured, he doesn't admit his mistakes and under values his enemies. Therefore, he is likely to face quite a few failures. However, an unexpected comeback is also in the cards!

Immigrants during the year of the **Dragon** are capable of anything in order to reach their goals. People evading totalitarian systems or enclosed societies could take on incredible threats in order to succeed, defying dangers and even risking their own lives. They will try to escape by any means, be it water, air or land; if caught, they will still push their fate. Their adopted land will allow them to reach the highest achievements. Unfortunately, few can keep up with a **Dragon** and his energy. He might defeat any partner, and his incendiary passions could burn everything around him to the ground and force him to end up alone in life. But, he will even face solitude successfully!

The native **Aries (March 21–April 19)** who immigrated during the year of the Dragon, is an impetuous fighter, and no matter how many difficulties arise, he faces them. He has no doubts about anything and prefers to act instinctively, with no consideration for the consequences of his actions. Since he can do no wrong, he would never learn from his mistakes. Fixed ideas could trap him in dangerous situations, sometimes of a financial nature. Should sentimental disappointments come his way, anger and thirst for revenge might get the better of him. He finds refuge in his work, in any activities for that matter, simply to occupy his mind and nourish him spiritually, making up for all the time he feels condemned to unhappiness.

Joseph Pulitzer, Hungarian-born journalist and editor, is among them.

Behind a shy and introverted façade, a **Taurus (April 20–May 20)** hides a volcanic temperament, ready to erupt at any moment, tormenting himself with his obsession for perfection. Life is a battle for him, and he throws in all he has to fight it. He is ambitious, organized, and stubborn, with great focus; nothing stands in his way should he set his mind on a target. However, he can also be a volcano randomly spitting out lava and energy. In his youth, he falls in love passionately, but he might not find the right life partner, someone who could appreciate his true qualities. Perhaps immigration during the year of the Dragon will let him find *the one*, the person able to share and respond in kind to him.

The **Gemini (May 21–June 20)** who immigrates in the year of the Dragon is permanently unsettled. He is always in search of happiness, fascinated by any novel area of interest in which he tries to make his mark, even without any qualifications! He sees himself as a pioneer, although this could derail into megalomania; he thinks he can succeed in anything he sets his mind on, anywhere and at any time. However, he gets bored easily, doesn't like repetition, which is why no routine job suits him. If an attractive prospect shows up somewhere else, be it in another country or continent, he is ready to emigrate again and again for it.

The **Cancer (June 21–July 22)** immigrant during the year of the Dragon does exactly what he wants to and bears the consequences. In his adoptive land he is in search of stability, which needs to be full of luxury. Born with a talent for finding the favorable settings, he always lives up to his dreams; it helps that he is also supported by influential people whom he wins over by pretending to be weak, playing on their need to protect less fortunate ones. A Cancer plays his *unfairness* card very well. In fact, he is very strong and resilient, even fighting against bouts of depression he may experience later in life. No matter how alienated he feels in his adopted country, he will never regret the decision to emigrate, although his native country might have brought him a fulfilling professional life.

Nothing could ignite more sparks than the combination between a **Leo (July 23–August 23)** and a Dragon! These two fire signs joined together could erupt in bursts of energy and vitality. The immigrant under their double occurrence could experience grandiose dreams and majestic plans, boundless courage and initiative, commanding respect without intimidation. He is not happy, but he is powerful. He bursts with adrenaline, making it difficult for others to put up with him. He is a social butterfly, but could end up alone, as he seeks controversy and provokes others. Monotony and quietude could simply suffocate him. He is active until late in life, looking for busy and exciting environments. Life in big energetic cities can satisfy his hunger for action.

The **Virgo (August 24–Sept 22)** who immigrates during the year of the Dragon enters his new country under a sign far more powerful than his birth one. This can shake and physically and emotionally destabilize him, in his adopted country. He needs prestige and recognition in life, wants to prove his potential and fundamentally change his mentality by starting up courageous projects. Unfortunately, these projects could prove to be too much for him in the end. He resorts to imagination to make up for the new reality he floats through on fresh energies. Unconventional sometimes. To prove his superiority, he could go into empirical or alternative science, practicing his spiritual force.

A **Libra (Sept 23–Oct 22)** native immigrated during the year of the Dragon is not particularly courageous, but extremely energetic and deliberate. Emigration occurs only after careful calculation of its risks and benefits; though once on his way, nothing can stop him. He brings along an infusion of fresh energy and love for action. He is entrepreneurial and inventive; he could come out a winner every time given his diplomacy and knack for persuasion. He is an apparently happy immigrant who reconciles himself to his adopted home.

A **Scorpio (Oct 23–Nov 21)** who immigrates in the year of the Dragon proves to be crazily courageous, ignoring any danger, limits or barriers. He secretly plans it all relying on himself only, and doesn't shy away from any kind of conflict, to reach his goals. However, he is emotionally weak and life's obstacles could get to him later in his years, enabling an alcohol or a drug addiction to overtake him. He has an inferiority complex towards the native more accomplished people in his adopted land. At the same time, he has a feeling of superiority, which helps him overcome his frustationsfrustrations. A dedicated parent, he always supports his kids, although he might not be fortunate in love.

A **Sagittarius (Nov 22–Dec 21)** immigrant during the year of the Dragon has a need for an active life, always busy, involved in important, long-term projects, even pro bono ones. The biggest enemy he has is inactivity which can bring with it useless and pessimistic feelings. All this is very dangerous to his personality, mainly in his mature years when the wish for channeling his energy into grandiose acts is overwhelming. His magnetic nature will draw admiration and followers. He is restless, inventive, with an endless imagination.

Serbian-born performance artist Marina Abramovic is in this group.

The **Capricorn (Dec 22–Jan 19)** native who immigrates during the year of the Dragon comes across as demanding, sometime even aggressive, though these feelings are all rooted in an ambition for perfection. He cannot stand failures from those closest to him; he is always in a quest for perfection and the absolute, driven by the wish to be the best in everything he touches. A straight-talker, he always speaks his mind, which can easily label him harsh or unlikable. The first years in his adopted country could be stormy, but time will bring accomplishments he wouldn't have dared to dream of in his native home.

A Dragon immigrant born an **Aquarius (Jan 20–Feb 18)** has a good nature, is loyal to his friends and is always ready to help them. Keeping busy and active, this immigrant loves to work and can very well make it in solitude, surrounded only by his hobbies and passions. In his adopted country, he can find spiritual fulfillment, given a good life partner who understands and respects him. On the other hand, he could very well just remain in his ivory tower if he doesn't find love.

The native **Pisces (Feb 19–Mar 20)** immigrated during the year of the Dragon stands out by his unexpected imagination. Some perceive him as an artist, others think him crazy. He is creative, but always ready to start a fight or fight back. As such, he could start conflicts, which in turn could energize his neurotic, restless, sometime destructive nature. He will continue to work into his late years, with a great passion for his labor.

YEAR OF THE
SNAKE

The year of the **Snake** could be marked by social change or political revolt, sometimes of a violent nature. Notably, the fall of Communism in Europe and September 11th in America happened during years of the **Snake**.

Immigrants during the year of the Snake are bound to go through major personal changes, which will only become evident after spending a while in their adopted country. Their emigration is not traumatic, although it might seem that way on the surface.

The **Snake**, lonely and distant, plans his emigration secretly, with intelligence and practicality. Cool and calculated, he doesn't lose his head easily. He *does* take managed risks and skillfully maneuvers through dangers.

In his adopted country, he insinuates himself into profitable professional organizations, ready to take control at the slightest weakness he perceives in the structure.

He also knows when to call it quits! If he achieves a decent and stable standard of living, he crawls under a warm stone and enjoys his siesta basking in his accomplishments.

An **Aries (Mar 21–Apr 19)** immigrated in the year of the Snake, faces great difficulties at the beginning of his new life, and, ultimately may not able to succeed. Although he faces up to life's challenges with courage and vitality, little by little his enthusiasm dies down. He therefore ends up choosing his battles and only does what he likes, avoiding social engagements. While he started out in life as an idealist, his later years are likely to transform him into a disillusioned wise man. On the other hand, he could have an exceptional destiny in the adopted country, transforming his deliberate solitude and cynicism into outstanding life accomplishments.

This was the case with the philosopher Emil Cioran, a Romanian-born who is considered one of the greatest French thinkers, a cynic praising loneliness and deception just to emphasize the miracle of life.

Sensual, sentimental and sensitive, the **Taurus (Apr 20–May 20)** who immigrates during the year of the Snake has difficulty in accepting the values of another culture. Instead, he carries nostalgia for his native home, which could push him to return to his birth country later in life. The concept of *home* resonates very strongly with the Snake-Taurus—stability as much as conservatism defines him—and is often mystified through his sentimental memory sweetening the past and keeping only the happy moments to remember.

Born under an air sign, the **Gemini (May 21–June 20)** who immigrated during the year of the Snake becomes more terrestrial. As such, he snakes into good professional careers, learning things as he goes. Although he seems easily adaptable, he does not fully, deeply, adapt to his new country. A winner by nature, he doesn't care to keep or protect his conquests. It all seems to slip away from him. He doesn't find motivation to stay in his birth place, or to remain in his adopted country. The sign of the Snake is only underscoring the pendulum motion between his two worlds, without letting him grow roots in either place.

Used to living in plush luxury, the **Cancer (June 21–July 22)** is an unpredictable immigrant, difficult to satisfy, elitist and introverted. He brings his routines and demands with him to his adopted country. Although his hopes might be crushed to start with, he waits for the favorable moment to come out of his shell and use any opportunity to satisfy his vanity and need for affluence. The Snake sign lends him toughness and accentuates his selfishness, both well hidden under a mask of thoughtfulness.

A **Leo** (**July 23–August 23**) who immigrates in the year of the Snake is chosen by destiny. The strength of the Leo combined with the wisdom of the Snake makes him a successful immigrant. Everything he touches turns to gold. This combination favors intellectuals. However, the Leo's need for laurels doesn't mesh well with the Snake's restraint or his urge for seclusion. Despite life-successes, this dichotomy could generate uncertainty and imbalance in his later years.

Fussy and contented, the **Virgo** (**Aug 24–Sept 22**) carefully analyzes the chances and risks that come with emigration. In fact, he would rather have a foreign country immigrate to him than take up the unknown. If he decides to immigrate during the year of the Snake, he only achieves professional peaks, not financial ones. When it comes to his personal life, he is a sensual partner, but difficult, demanding and erratic. In his adopted country, he ends up unhappy, the grass is always greener on the other side for him.

Although a **Libra (Sept 24–Oct 22)** immigrates only after giving it a lot of thought, in his adopted land, he is not able to shake off the feeling that he made the wrong decision. However, the paradoxical combination between his social, happy, chatty and pleasant nature, and the meditative and quiet Snake, somehow creates a beneficial setting for his in the new country. He will finally find his balance.

Among all the western zodiac signs, the **Scorpio (Oct 23–Nov 21)** best resembles the Snake. Therefore, the native Scorpio who immigrates during the year of the Snake does not experience a significant change of destiny. His personality also remains basically unchanged, mysterious, intuitive. He is essentially a hermit who chooses exactly the right moment to lunge into a calculated and unscrupulous attack. There is also a chance he could fall victim to his own imprudence.

Extravagant and idealist, adventurous and an enthusiast, the **Sagittarius (Nov 22–Dec 21)** didn't grow strong roots in his native home, which, in turn, helps him not to look back with nostalgia and sentimentalism.

His destiny is the open road, liberty and independence. While he used to shoot for the stars, immigration during the year of the Snake might transform him into a more terrestrial person, forced to accept compromises. Nevertheless, he still gazes at the skies, even if he lives under a rock.

Wise, cold and calculating, introspective and enigmatic, a **Capricorn (Dec 22–Jan 19)** perfectly supports the sign of the Snake. After a stormy youth, he devotes himself to his professional life and enjoys remarkable triumphs in his adopted country. He is inflexible, polite, and serious to the point of lacking any humor and sounding aged. It might take a while for him to adapt to his new home, but once he does, he comes out of hiding. Immigration stimulates his ambition of showing how he can do anything he sets his mind to, and, paradoxically, the anxieties brought on by new beginnings helps him find his emotional balance.

An **Aquarius (Jan 20–Feb 19)** immigrated during the year of the Snake winds through dangers quite tenaciously, is flexible and able to easily adapt to any circumstance in his new country. In a powerful, thought-provoking and emotional setting, he easily molds himself into any shape or form. Nonetheless, if he is ignored, he could lash out in ruthless attack. Discreet and mysterious, he comes across as very charming, attractive and witty. He enjoys friends' company, but equally cherishes his solitary moments. One could label him a serene immigrant, content with his destiny.

In his adopted country, although malleable and adaptable, a **Pisces (Feb 19–March 20)** immigrant in the year of the Snake is more like a fish *out* of water, than swimming like a snake *in* the water. Without being courageous, he enjoys shocking and gathering praise from people. If attacked, he absorbs the hits and turns them against his enemies. He is obstinate in trying to lead and make his voice heard, but he is lacking leadership qualities. Sometime extravagant or snobbish, he lives grandiosely and on the edge.

YEAR OF THE
HORSE

The horse is one of the animals that can be "born under a lucky star."

The year of the **Horse** is auspicious for immigration. Not only does it reward the talented, hard-working and ambitious immigrants, but it also offers reversals of fate in their adopted country which come along with unexpected financial gains.

Strong willed natures, unconventional and with special abilities, the immigrants in the Year of the **Horse** dream about pulling the world further and further towards exceptional accomplishments. They are always on the move, cannot stand any obstruction, political or of any other nature. Their destiny is to run unrestricted.

This immigrant chases success, and finds it in his second life. He is drawn to freedom, while remaining a traditionalist, nostalgic for his ancestral home, close to nature and ready, at any moment, to turn back time if only to prove to himself he made the right decision to leave, break away, part with everything and everyone who would have obstructed his ascension.

Dynamic, charming and social, hardworking but conceited, the **Horse** emigrant expects his merits to be publically recognized. He is a sore loser, considers himself always the rightful winner and a born leader. Except he has the making of a dictator.

He loves liberty and freedom and would like to lead crowds of people towards the light at the end of the tunnel, but only on his terms.

The **Aries (Mar 21–Apr 19)** immigrated during the year of the Horse is hardworking and determined, but not uninterested in rewards and recognition. He chooses emigration for economic reasons, striving to surpass the standard of living he had in his birthplace. Impatient and agitated, he may become disheartened if success is delayed. He quickly flies off the handle, especially with the weak and easily manipulated people, if it wasn't for the presence of the ones he likes to seduce or use. If his leadership qualities are in question, he could turn spiteful and vengeful.

The **Taurus (Apr 20–May 20)**, organized, methodical and tenacious, is, above all, very conservative and a traditionalist who hates change. Immigration transforms him into a materialistic person, eager to accumulate more and more wealth in order to secure a good life in his adopted country. He loves his new home and desperately tries to adapt to it. The year of the Horse turns him into a long distance runner, who looks over his shoulder at his past without regrets. He is loyal and persistent, willing to make it through impossible situations. In the end, his patience will be rewarded.

The **Gemini** immigrant (**May 21–Jun 20**) has, just like the Horse, a need for freedom and open space, is active, easily adaptable and is comfortable in any setting, anywhere in the world. Immigration means only a change of scenery for him—not at all a traumatic event. While he is easily fired up, he also gets bored quickly, has no trouble finding good jobs, and no trouble losing them. His suitcase waits for him by the doorway; he is always ready to pick up and fly away. He doesn't grow roots anywhere, because he believes that the grass is greener next door. He is sensitive, attracted by art and beauty.

American-born painter Mary Cassatt is part of this group.

A **Cancer** (**June 21–July 22**) longs for stability in life, needs to be with people stronger than himself, to belong with someone. However, he is as temperamental and finicky as the Horse, and that ultimately leaves him lonely, in a solitude he detests. Once more, just like the Horse, he is monopolizing and selfish, and, if criticized, could become unpleasant. If wounded, he crawls inside his shell and only comes out at the right moment, unexpectedly virulent. In his adopted country he might start out by being heavily in debt; his luck comes late in life, when he finds peace and restore his finances.

The **Leo** (**July 23–Aug 23**) is just like the Horse when it comes to his need for performance and the winners' podium, applause, honors and decoration. Unfortunately, he is also as vain as the Horse, which makes it difficult for the two of them to reign over the same kingdom. A Leo born again under the sign of the Horse might have to give up his laurels for the freedom to move around. However, the urge for success stays with him, and in his adopted country, he does at least make his wishes come true, if not actually lead as he had dreamed. He will always be able to pretend and look more important than he actually is.

Virgo natives (**Aug 24–Sept 22**) pluck up courage to emigrate, it is a difficult decision to try their luck in a new space, but they continue to hope that something will erase the shadows of the past and open up a bright future. However, they don't adapt easily anywhere. Virgos become sharp critics of the new world, finding that they face more trouble than they bargained for and dream of running away once again. The year of the Horse confers a touch of adventure on them. They might change life partners or professions, and always remain skeptical when it comes to happiness. Time turns their candor into cynicism, while hypochondria and anxieties end up being considered part of the unfriendly atmosphere in their adopted land—which they dream of leaving.

To be born a **Libra (Sept 23–Oct 22)** and become a Horse by immigration is a twist of fate, fortunately a lucky one. Thanks to his knack for social gathering, his enthusiasm and optimism, adapting to the new world comes easily and naturally. He has dilemmas and is hesitant to choosing or changing, but when he makes up his mind, he will go till the end. A Libra is the immigrant who can convince anybody of anything. He manages to be a maestro of communication, even when he isn't quite fluent in the local language.

Immigration brands a **Scorpio (Oct 23–Nov 21)** impulsive and conceited. Under the sign of the Horse, he succeeds professionally in the new world. However, he doesn't have many friends. Although charismatic, he often blunders and could offend without apologizing.

He is infatuated, sometimes even with a touch of mendacity; nonetheless, when he plans to seduce someone, he can look very well-educated, sensual and—for a short time—generous. Once the target is hit, he returns to his selfish and tough persona. His life always has a dark side in his adopted country as much as it did in his native home.

Drawn to freedom, a **Sagittarius (Nov 22–Dec 21)** emigrates without a blink. He is always ready to look back in time to prove to himself he made the right choice in departing, breaking away, evading enclosed societies and places where he couldn't breathe anymore and couldn't fly high. His need for independence and adventure matches the year of the Horse best. A Sagittarius, a half-horse himself, keeps on shooting for the stars, even though the sky might seem farther up in his adoptive land. Some people in this group could have quite an exceptional run.

The Romanian-born writers Eugen Ionescu and Andrei Codrescu are in this group.

A **Capricorn (Dec 22–Jan 19)** who immigrates during the year of the Horse is ambitious and pragmatic and uses his intelligence to find favorable situations to profit from. He chases success and actually achieves a bit of it, but only later in life. Selfish, just like any Horse, he has trouble sharing the fruits of his labor. Few Capricorn immigrants have a wish to emigrate back to their native country. It isn't easy for them to pull away, but when they do, their departures are final. They don't hold any grudge and look back without regrets; they are generally lucky, and immigration will favor their accomplishments.

The **Aquarius (Jan 20–Feb 18)** is less generous after immigration, and not a doer anymore. Instead, under the sign of the Horse, he wants to lead and be listened to, becomes dynamic and impulsive, eager to conquer the new world he entered, filled with hope and ideals. His revolutionary spirit defines him in the new country, makes him be perceived as a nonconformist. Swimming against the current, he tries to impose his views which are often in conflict with authoritative powers. However, he is not an anarchist. He knows when to stop, so as not to endanger his position and interests.

Albanian-born writer Ismail Kadare is in this group.

A **Pisces (Feb 19–Mar 20)** native who immigrates in the year of the Horse feels at home in his new country, although he might end up less accomplished professionally or financially than in his home. He is dedicated to his family, and for that reason he finds resources to stay and be satisfied with his partial accomplishments. Nonetheless, in his later years he might experience more bouts of anger and dissatisfaction. He could be unpleasant in certain social circles where he insists on shining. He could even grow aggressive or brutal if he feels as if he's losing a stake in something, or simply wants to impress. Always expecting honors, nothing pleases him more than exaggerated praise or heads bowed in respect around him.

YEAR OF THE
SHEEP

Immigrants during the year of the **Sheep**, sometimes also called the year of the **Goat**, can make do with anything. They will live through hardships at the beginning and ask very little from life, although they love wealth and luxury.

Their professional and material endeavors have highs and lows. While they emigrated as idealists, life transforms them into pragmatic souls.

A **Sheep** immigrant is intelligent, sensitive and contemplative. Not the active or entrepreneurial kind, he is rather a procrastinator, often finding solace in his own inertia. He has bursts of energy, followed by comfortable downtime.

His chance for success in life is to partner with someone stronger. Luckily, most of the time, his gut feeling guides him towards a life at ease.

A native **Aries (Mar 21–Apr 19)** who immigrated in the year of the Sheep starts his new life tumultuously, with big dreams, but in time his energy will fade away little by little. It is even likely his professional life will decline and he ends up lazy and inactive. Throughout it all, he is still able to find ways to satisfy his needs, perhaps good sponsors or a life partner willing to keep him going. He spreads himself too thin, and the Sheep traits only stress his shallowness.

A **Taurus (Apr 20–May 20)** is a hard worker, stable and tenacious. No challenge is too big for him. He decides to be assimilated into *the new world*, even if it means giving up his routine. The sign of the Sheep helps soften him, although leaving him as stubborn as always. While a Taurus is reserved and quiet, the Sheep is shy and has an inferiority complex: the immigrant who lands this combination is a shy person aging quietly and modestly. He will hardly be noticed by others, but will leave a legacy behind.

Born a **Gemini (May 21–June 20)**, therefore under an air sign, this immigrant does not change his personality: he remains the most flexible immigrant, although also indecisive. Emigration is an easy task for the Gemini. Social butterflies, charming and seductive in society, well-mannered and brilliant conversation partners, the Geminis who immigrated in the year of the Sheep know how to make themselves admired. They don't seek out routine desk-jobs as they dislike sitting for too long or undergoing sustained effort. Instead, they use their charm to forge relationships with people who could help them get easy and well-paid jobs. Speculative and optimistic by nature, they keep up their Gemini duality through their new destiny as an immigrant, borrowing from the Sheep's traits of procrastination and indecisiveness.

Born a romantic, a dreamer and a spoiled soul, a **Cancer (June 21–July 22)** can't wait to emigrate to have something to complain about! The year of the Sheep serves his whims and elitist attitude very well, making him an even bigger spender than he used to be in his native land. He still lacks the means to pay his bills. He is somehow able to find people whose hearts he breaks as he makes them pay his debts. A vain person, he seeks to rise up in his new society. Often, defiantly, he hides his true colors. He has a sharp complex mind, and, just like the Sheep, he is extremely sensitive to critics. This immigrant is strong and possesses unexpected resources. In his adoptive country, he chooses the winding road, doesn't shine professionally, but is able to somehow, surprisingly, survive. Just when you expect him at the bottom of the ocean, he waves at you from the top of a mountain!

A **Leo** (**July 23–Aug 23**) native who immigrated during the year of the Sheep tries to dominate and rule his adopted country rather than become tamed by it. Arrogant and sure of himself, greedy for honors and grandeur, he seeks out high-level positions which could satisfy his vanity while also generously compensate him financially. Immigration during the year of the Sheep adds perseverance to his natural superiority complex, making him able to repeat attacks over and over again, hoping to achieve successful outcomes. However, he gets bored easily. He is in fact used to conquering and devouring energies, incapable of stability in life. He protects his family, but could also go into bouts of rage if they don't rise to his expectations. Starting out in life extremely arrogant, he could turn into a cynical, impatient person later on, only to end up depressed, because his accomplishments did not shine as brightly as he thinks they should have.

The **Virgo (Aug 24–Sept 22),** born a meticulous dogmatic perfectionist, becomes even more circumspect when when immigrating during the year of the Sheep. Always unsatisfied, even pessimistic, he lives with a nostalgia for his place of birth, continuously trying to recreate the universe of his childhood and youth. Forever he will feel insecure and threatened by the unknown, tormented by doubts and hungry for stability in life. His analytic mind will sharpen. Wherever he ends up emigrating to, he seeks to feel the ground under his feet. Nevertheless, he will always think of himself as being uprooted, unadaptable and ready in a flash to return to his native country.

A **Libra (Sept 24–Oct 22)** dislikes solitude and hates being isolated from people, always looking for companionship in social circles. He makes for a great mediator in human relations, knows how to settle conflicts, and is ready to help anytime anywhere. His natural need for balance makes him oscillate and hesitant. A Libra has a hard time deciding to do something, only to easily change his mind afterwards. Immigration during the year of the Sheep accentuates his interior imbalance; he looks for stability in a life partner, while staying alert to any possible change outside his circle. However, he doesn't finalize any outlandish intention, flirting being enough for him, in fact. Although he dislikes risk, his adopted country will sometimes force him to take them.

Elie Wiesel is among them.

The **Scorpio (Oct 23–Nov 21)** native is reborn in his adopted country, pushing his limits and optimizing his destiny. His natural shrewdness, combined with intuition—a trait he shares with the Sheep—makes him indestructible. Passionate, indiscreet by nature, he adores secrets but cannot keep them; therefore, he cannot be a spy, although he loves spying. He is a sharp critic, a generous lover, an amusing partner, hiding his weaknesses. He is easily adaptable to anything anywhere, while patiently staking out opportunities that can bring him great advantage.

A **Sagittarius (Nov 22–Dec 20)**, a freedom and adventure lover, emigrates without giving it much thought and adapts to the new world effortlessly, thanks to his flexibility and tolerance. Not as open and social as arrogant, he often confuses humor with irony, and that can make him uncomfortable in a society that doesn't have an understanding for his type. However, this immigrant is influenced by the kindness and sincerity of the Sheep.

He will therefore become less narcissistic and more of a negotiator, looking to obtain independence in social standing that would bring him stability.

A **Capricorn (Dec 22–Jan 19),** wise and enigmatic, introverted and pessimistic, cold and deliberate, this sign needs a big push to emigrate. But once he does take the step, he won't look back, although given his strong sense of values, he will keep memories of his native country close. Cautious and thrifty, he lives under the constant fear of going to the poorhouse. Extremely ambitious, he succeeds professionally, slowly but surely; once accomplished, he carefully takes all protective measures he can to hold on to his hard-sought accomplishments. The year of the Sheep is not too beneficial to a Capricorn native. He could easily have bouts of rage, just like the soft-hearted Sheep, while his sensitivity is likely to slip into irascibility. Although a fatalist, he makes it into old age, even though his life comes to pass under the constant fear of death.

The native **Aquarius (Jan 20–Feb 18),** altruistic and generous, closely tied to his family and friends, devotes himself to humanitarian causes and carries his idealism mindfully. Easily adaptable and good-natured, immigration in the year of the Sheep becomes an easy task for him, in spite of the financial difficulties of a new beginning. The new life allows him to find support mechanisms, if not professional then through the care of his children and life partner. However, he may go through psychological lows, becoming vulnerable if treated harshly, or if he finds his trust betrayed.

The native **Pisces (Feb 19–Mar 20)** who immigrates in the year of the Sheep, is constantly in search of his identity. He is uprooted and continuously tries to recreate the atmosphere of his native land, in the hope of finding the balance and stability needed to keep on going. However, being unstable and difficult by birth, he has a tough time finding peace. Even when things seem to work out fine, he finds reasons to be unsatisfied. In his adopted country, he could find himself swimming like a fish in water, but must stay away from strong currents. He seeks to be his own master, avoiding partnerships in work or business.

YEAR OF THE
MONKEY

Immigrants who change during the year of the **Monkey** come into the full arsenal of seduction and manipulation displayed by this lucky and intelligent animal, an arsenal that can be used to reach personal goals anywhere life may lead. His new destiny changes fundamentally, entering under the incidence of a two-faced sign which pushes him into risky activities, extravagant changes, unusual undertakings, often with an unexpected ending.

Immigrants during the year of the **Monkey** have presence of mind, curiosity, courage and a knack for easy adaptability to anything anywhere, which greatly helps them in their adopted country. Unfortunately, since they sometimes think their ideas are the best in the world and get stuck on them, they may suffer the consequences of having too much self-assurance.

Experts in the art of dissimulation, they are very preoccupied to project a good image of themselves and fend off any failure. Dynamic and full of initiative, they may go far on the professional ladder in their adopted home.

An **Aries (Mar 21–Apr 19)** uses his natural initiative to take full advantage of the beneficent traits of the playful Monkey, only he is even more disorganized than he used to be, spreading himself too thin doing useless projects and leaving important ventures unfinished. Nonetheless, his dynamism and spontaneity guides him to make the right choices, and, if he is able to control his impulsive nature, he might end up a winner after all.

A **Taurus (Apr 20–May 20)** doesn't have much in common with the temperament and personality of the Monkey. He detests playing monkey tricks, has no passion for amusement, and doesn't know how to pretend or be playful. Emigration traumatizes him, turning his universe and values upside down. He could find refuge in food (being a gourmand) or in books (not at all the athletic type), but he does remain continuously discontent in his adopted country where he feels that his talents are not as recognized and appreciated as they deserve to be. Against all odds, emigration in a year of the Monkey might turn him into a melancholic personality, someone who prefers to be isolated and meditative rather than mingle with the crowd.

The year of the Monkey is the ideal sign for immigration of **Gemini (May 21–June 20)** natives. This year resonates perfectly with their flexible duplicitous nature, quick reaction and sharp minds. Their actions, paradoxical and risky, border on legality, just like the Monkey's. They enjoy a life of pleasure, ready at a moment's notice to risk everything for a night of fun times. Not at all concerned with the consequences of their actions, these immigrants have trouble taking responsibility in life; however, being good communicators, they are able to convince anybody of anything. They emigrate out of curiosity. If success doesn't come quickly and effortlessly, they may look for something else. Gemini are in constant movement and can easily squeeze through crowds. The sign of the Monkey fits a Gemini like a glove. There will always be a branch he can grab on to, swinging playfully.

For the accomplishments in his adopted country, a **Cancer (June 21–July 22)** who immigrated in the year of the Monkey we'll be applauded and honored. He plays humble, waiting for his merits to be recognized. He has no trouble taking responsibility for his mistakes, is an enthusiastic supporter of the community and could be a good leader if opportunity occurs. He is generous and ready to help others; dedicates his life to serving the truth. If he faces unfair criticism, he will get out of his shell and fight back.

Greek-born author and businesswoman Ariana Huffington is among them.

A sign combination of great success is the **Leo** (**July 23–Aug 23**) who immigrates in the year of the Monkey. His luck doubles, along with his professional and material accomplishments. The adopted country turns out to be an ideal stage for him. His need for grandeur is completely satisfied. He becomes a perfect patron, a leader projecting his force through the flexibility and resourcefulness borrowed from the Monkey. From the Monkey, he also learns ways to circumvent the law if need be on his way to grow his influence or wealth. In spite of his success—which calls forth plenty of resentment—he is not a happy winner, doesn't know when to quit and will not be able to enjoy the fruits of his labor.

A **Virgo** (**Aug 24–Sept 22**) instinctively avoids immigration during a year of the Monkey, a sign he has very little in common with. However, if that happens, he always feels left behind, uncomfortable, irritable and unsatisfied. His destiny is twisted. He has an identity crisis and develops an aversion to other well-adapted immigrants. Turned into an anxious person, he looks for an appropriate moment to make his return trip to his native land, wishing to emigrate again under a better sign, in a time that would confer stability upon his new life.

A **Libra** (**Aug 24–Sept 22**) has no problem swinging from the same branch with a Monkey, especially if the latter helps curtail useless oscillations and balances him. Born with a positive attitude, energetic and enthusiastic, this Monkey-Libra immigrant easily fluctuates from happiness to sadness. He can be the perfect winner if he finds security in his new life and a supportive partner.

A **Scorpio** (**Oct 23–Nov 21**) who immigrates during the year of the Monkey is attracted by strange experiences, and his original character blooms. Whimsical, egocentric and used to having it all, he embraces his second destiny naturally, easily adapts to the dynamics of his new home and falls in love with it because he is now able to enjoy a higher standard of living. He knows how to shield himself from tough challenges, has sound instincts while staying alert, and is always ready to attack in order to protect his gains or his public image.

A **Sagittarius (Nov 22–Dec 21)** who immigrates during a year of the Monkey doesn't make the best choice. His defects, rather than his good qualities, are enhanced. Cunning and versed, the Monkey knows how to bring out an unfounded optimism in the Sagittarius, which would include, bragging, speculation and narcissism (even when combined with an artistic nature) and generosity at others' expense. Everything is confused, chaotic, but with a sense of humor. A generally pleasant and likable Sagittarius, could, under the Monkey's influence, change into an arrogant and contemptuous person.

Just like any other horned animal, a native **Capricorn (Dec 22–Jan 19)** remains ambitious and stubborn, difficult to manipulate. The Monkey is the only one able to deceive or divert him from his path, incite him into fantasies or extravagance, encourage him to take the road less traveled, all by overwhelming him with praise and gifts. The immigrant in this group needs time to get used to the tensions and challenges launched by the Monkey, but, if he manages to do that, he ends up a winner for the rest of his life.

Given his native contagious optimism, inventiveness and need for strong emotions, an **Aquarius (Jan 20– Feb 18)** could find great success under the sign of the Monkey. No matter how difficult or absurd a setting is, an Aquarius finds an original solution and comes up with an explanation (be it paradoxical at times) for it all; if the Monkey won't stick his nose into it, he will definitely convince everybody that he is right.

If a native **Pisces (Feb 19–Mar 20),** unsettled and unpredictable, jumps into the deep waters of immigration during a year of the Monkey, he is then floating on favorable currents towards success, from the very beginning. Without being the courageous type, he is capable of extravagant gestures and counts on favorable opportunities. Just like the Monkey, he wants to make a good impression at any cost, and is ready to juggle anything around just to be admired. His luck makes up for his inability in business. The duplicity of Pisces, supported by that of the Monkey's, could push him into a life of having a split personality.

YEAR OF THE
ROOSTER

The emigrant during the year of the **Rooster** is able to find the best solution without taking many risks or accepting compromises. He likes clear-cut settings and situations he can keep under control. Rather than crossing the border hidden in a car trunk, he would negotiate with the border patrol. And he not only may be able to convince the border patrol that his actions are necessary but can also gain favors or cause impossible embarrassment to others. He is a talented orator, with a remarkable power of persuasion and magnetism. His adopted country offers him many opportunities, as he is a hard worker, diligent and fully aware of his own resources.

Very rarely would an immigrant during the year of the **Rooster** become depressed or alienated! Not only is he able to recreate himself, accepting any challenge, but he also has the power to awake in others a wish or enthusiasm to strive for the better and to uncover unknown talents inside themselves. In as much as he was riotous in his native land, he becomes a diplomat in his adopted country. However, once he tests the waters in his new country, he regains his voice and makes himself heard so as to awaken fresh energies in people close to him.

The **Rooster** marches tall through his own destiny, his rooster's comb up high. He is indeed a spurred rooster sharpening up to face difficulties which he is confident to overcome. He will neutralize his adversaries with clever words. Just give him the opportunity to fight face-to-face in a cock-fight.

The **Aries (Mar 21–Apr 19)** who immigrates during the year of the Rooster starts out forcefully, trumpeting his courage around, strong willed and hard working. However, time slows him down, although he remains on the same social level. He is tolerant and generous, but has trouble getting close to people or allowing himself be figured-out by others. At the same time, he could hold a grudge and dislike people who compete with him professionally, or who intend to challenge his authority. A bragger, just like the Rooster, he can be very vociferous if his merits are not recognized, but would only make his voice heard in a setting he can control. In general, he is a pleasant presence, inspires confidence, only rarely losing his self-confidence, even if the immigration dream doesn't come true for him.

A **Taurus (Apr 20–May 20)** who immigrates during the year of the Rooster confronts his destiny. He enjoys such confrontations, draws energy from them and keeps his mind alert. If he is provoked, he reacts promptly. He fights openly and directly. An imposing, robust person, he has complicated thoughts. Under the sign of the Rooster, he sharpens his sense of critique, and his intelligence and tenacity helps him find exciting challenging companionship. Though pleasant and well meaning, he can also grow sarcastic with people who defy him. Sensuality filters everything for him, while physical attraction plays a central role, and therefore situations can sometimes reverse themselves.

Russian-born songwriter Irving Berlin is among them.

If a native of **Gemini (May 21–June 20)** decides to immigrate, illegally, during the year of the Rooster, he could have a rough time. He is used to finding the round-about, unconventional way to solve problems—risky or bordering legality—all of which are rather more in step with the nature of a Monkey than a Rooster. Good instincts can however lead Gemini to travel back and forth a number of times, he finds the favorable moment for immigration, a moment and a place to accept him just as he is. Charming and speculative, Gemini show off their knowledge, as superficial as it may be. All that makes him sound similar to the Rooster, except that the latter is hardworking with perseverance. If a Rooster shows off his knowledge, it is only to impress his entourage (like the Gemini), however his information would have been gathered carefully before delivery (unlike the Gemini).

A **Cancer (June 21–July 22)** would only immigrate to a place where there is food on the table and his bed is made. He doesn't like to take risks, courage is not his strongest suit; he goes with the flow, wishing for novelty and adventure. Though the adventure needs to be well-planned and comfortable! Shy and prudent, a Cancer who immigrates during the year of the Rooster enters a more energetic sign, which he copes with very well though, as he always does, hiding under a shield of weakness. The Rooster and the Cancer have limited temperamental compatibility: while the first one is obsessed with continuously moving forward, pragmatic and always in action, the latter is tempted to stay in one place, contemplative and snobbish. The Cancer native might come out of this dynamic combination with hard to control anxieties. He is, however, similar to the Rooster in being quite critical and wanting to have the last word.

A **Leo (July 23–Aug 23)** who immigrates during the year of the Rooster makes a great choice: he fulfills his destiny in his adopted country and lives as intensely as he always did. A Leo reigns over the wilderness and its animals, while the Rooster's kingdom is the backyard of a home. They are equally respected, feared and appreciated, fond of honors and recognition. While a Leo is born a leader, the Rooster is a great administrator. The Leo sees the big picture, while the Rooster pays attention to the details. They are both good, talented, fighters who gain everyone's respect. Even their enemies admire them. Not that they have much of a choice! The Rooster-Leo is a weird champion, with claws, comb and wings. He inspires respect and is capable of generosity after his own vanity is satisfied. The sense of being superior will always stay with him, even if in his late years he might secretly hide and lick his sentimental wounds.

An immigrant born a **Virgo (Aug 24–Sept 22)** only gains energy under the sign of the Rooster. With his feet solidly planted on the ground, a Virgo doesn't like to take chances or complicate his life. He prefers to know whom exactly he is dealing with and who he can count on. His emigration is carefully planned so as to cause minimal trauma and risk. The Rooster satisfies his need for perfection, encouraging it to keep and enhance his analytical and innermost intelligence. A Virgo doesn't accept mistakes, superficiality and amateurish natures in others. He is rigid and critical. However, the psychological make-up of man vs. woman in a Virgo is quite different. The male Virgo has an appetite for catastrophe, philosophy, and is a cold, introverted, cynical person. The woman, under a mask of fragility, is meticulous and hard working. Both the man and woman have a somewhat bored demeanor. And sometimes they are boring. Even the Rooster, with all his bursts of effusion cannot put a dent in it all.

A **Libra (Sept 23–Oct 22)** thinks long and hard about the decision to emigrate. If he chooses to immigrate during the year of the Rooster, he can find the stability he always longed for. If the Libra native is deliberate when it comes to money, the sign of the Rooster makes him even more sparing. However, he despises people calling him stingy. His success in the adopted country is proof you can live without overindulging, be well-balanced, and have an optimistic view on life. He knows how to avoid risks and minimize losses; with a positive and chatty personality, he is tolerant and open, prudent, bordering on sometimes being afraid, although nothing can stop his professional growth.

The **Scorpio (Oct 23–Nov 21)** shuts himself off from the world, wherever he lands in his immigration. He decides to keep a low profile, is private and solitaire although he used to be very popular in his native land. Being cynical in order to hide his emotions, or looking down upon others when he feels superior intellectually—neither helps his likability. Although born under a water sign, he doesn't adapt easily once he is taken from his entourage. Conceited and proud, just like a Rooster, he will build himself an artificial universe, a protective shield, and will pretend to the world that he has adapted perfectly.

The **Sagittarius (Nov 22–Dec 21)** who immigrates during the year of the Rooster holds on to his ideals, but now aims lower and closer to himself. After showing off his organizational and administrative talents, intensified by the influence of the Rooster, he finds a secure, cozy place to retreat to, away from the limelight. He likes to fool himself, and easily confabulates. Having an overflowing imagination, he is quick to grasp ideas, seems to be a know-it-all, and sometimes comes across as arrogant and conceited. His love for nature and trips won't change, as he is ready at a moment's notice to launch into a new project or jump on a plane toward an unusual destination.

Capricorns (Dec 22–Jan 19) are neither idealists, nor utopians. They emigrate only after careful planning, and most of the time they don't regret what was left behind. If things don't turn out the way they wanted, their ambition and stubbornness will transform them into tenacious fighters, capable of reversing a bad situation. Nothing comes easy to Rooster-Capricorn immigrants. They work hard for everything they accomplish and can't stand failure, whether it happens to them or to those close to them. They are selfish but generous at heart, thrifty but take things on impulsively. Yet time is on their side.

An **Aquarius (Jan 20–Feb 18)** who immigrates during the year of the Rooster always remains an idealist. No matter where he ends up or how much he has accomplished, his most treasured possession is always stays with him: words. Curious and hungry for knowledge, he could spend his life in a secluded room filled with only books. He is an accomplished orator and can talk for hours about anything to anyone. If forced to leave his ivory tower in order to offer help, he does it with generosity and altruism. However, too much contact with the real world may threaten his stability.

The **Pisces** native (**Feb 19–Mar 20**) who immigrated during the year of the Rooster could make it to the top. He is a very energetic fighter, impetuous and extremely inventive, and takes all the challenges his second life may throw at him. And wins. Moreover, he himself incites the new world, through novel ideas and discoveries. He is a pioneer, the voice of new beginnings, able to start revolutions. What better example of this group than Albert Einstein!

YEAR OF THE
DOG

Immigrants who move to new countries during the year of the **Dog** have their lucky star to thank for their decision. They easily adapt to their new world, respecting its rules and laws. The new country grows on them, while their tolerant and liberal nature turns them into devoted and patriotic citizens, even if all their dreams don't come true.

Idealists, these immigrants look to change the world at the intellectual level. Meditative and preoccupied by the profound meaning of human existence, they can sometimes be quite pessimistic, with bouts of anxiety, especially in the second part of their lives. They do, however, bury all that in their daily work.

Modest by nature, they are resourceful enough to live away from the hustle-and-bustle of the world.

Thorough and passionate in their endeavors, inventive and original, creative and energetic, they may be lucky enough to become accomplished and as recognized as they deserve in their new home.

The **Aries** native (**Mar 21–Apr 19**) who immigrates during the year of the Dog becomes much more organized, managing his impulsiveness. If he used to spread himself too thin and get bored about it all very quickly, he is now able to complete his endeavors, in spite of his impetuosity and die-hard bad habits. Very much like the Dog, he takes pride in keeping his word; immigration proves beneficial for him all around. Marked by a need for change and obsessed by trying to optimize the universe, his native talent or sheer strength brightens his star in life, making it shine brilliantly. Charlie Chaplin is one of these immigrants who reached such outstanding peaks.

A **Taurus** (**Apr 20–May 20**), stubborn and one-minded, is a slow learner who never forgets. Defined by his memory and loyalty—the latter being the main characteristic of the Dog also, this immigrant follows his destiny without deviating much from his original course. Although he can turn furious, as bad as can be, he would stop dead in his tracks at the sight of a flower in his way and smell it tenderly: he *is* Disney's *Ferdinand the Taurus*, sentimental and disarmed. His personality will soften up under the sign of the Dog. His stiffness will become a bit more malleable and he will grow into a more tolerant person, without some of his old prejudices.

Here we have a native of **Gemini (May 21–June 20)** as curious and intelligent as the Dog. Under this sign, he grudgingly reformulates his destiny, forced as he is to play by the rules and give up his whims, now able to embark on long-lasting difficult projects. He is unpredictable, can always surprise you with his choices, but he can thank his lucky stars and sound instincts that protect him from disasters. Optimistic and enjoying some bravado, he will never admit to his close-calls, pretending to have only explored the "dark side of the moon."

Immigration under the sign of the Dog is quite a provocation for a **Cancer (June 21–July 22)** native, unaccustomed to make sacrifices or react in the face of failure. He turns his shyness into a weapon and uses it to buy compassion and sympathy from strangers eager to help him dispel pessimism. The Cancer is tenacious and shoots higher: little by little, on the sly, he will climb to the podium. Shy, but determined.

The winning emigration ticket could be in the paws of the **Leo** (**July 23–Aug 23**), immigrated during the year of the Dog. His strength and overflowing creativity need large spaces and freedom to manifest themselves. Unwilling to compromise, self-confident and ready to fight to the end, even if it is just to satisfy his vanity, this immigrant has great expectations and has the power to actually make it there. He can be extremely demanding and conceited. However, the vanity of the champion doesn't inconvenience anybody. He is grateful to the people who helped him immigrate in the beginning and always cherishes and values their relationships.

The **Virgo** (**Aug 24–Sept 22**), analytical by nature, carefully studies the risks and benefits of emigration. Just like the Dog, he always looks to optimize his destiny. In a continuous strive for perfection, whether he is in his native land or in his adopted home, he is an honest and judicial person who ends up hiding his disappointments under melancholy. Docile and conciliatory, he is shy and secluded in the beginning, only to impetuously launch out to make his dreams come true as soon as he feels grounded in his new home.

The most difficult task for a **Libra (Sept 23–Oct 22)** is to make a choice. Though once he does choose, he doesn't waiver in his pursuit, all the way to the end. Although he may not win the emigration war, he does win each one-on-one battle, with his diplomacy and natural tolerance—the sign of the Dog enhances these qualities conferring him stability and balance. Even though he is satisfied with the financial status reached in his adoptive country, he harbors regrets remembering his past financial blunders. A hopeless sentimentalist, even late in life!

The native **Scorpio (Oct 23–Nov 21)** who immigrates during the year of the Dog has a lot of trouble adapting to his new place. He holds resentment for those who succeed better than he has, while having difficulty controlling his extravagant whims. He looks for social environments conducive for him to display his knowledge and be perceived as superior. Professionally, he is drawn to jobs requiring little to no human interaction. He may shine as a researcher, scholar, a keeper of records or computer specialist.

A **Sagittarius (Nov 22–Dec 21)** has a lot in common with the Dog: an honest fighter, with a sincere and open nature. He is guided in life by truth and properness, even when he makes mistakes. However, he has a talent for self-delusion. He is skillful in exaggerating and living in his own world, and that could ease his immigration trauma while hurting his own feelings. When reality is too much for him, he resorts to speculation and philosophy. He is the immigrant who is content in both homes, smartly and gracefully oscillating between them, with no feeling of alienation.

Energetic and with a tireless capacity to work, a **Capricorn (Dec 22–Jan 19)** immigrant holds on to his ambition to break into high society; his successes in his adopted country are due to his unrelenting eagerness and tenacity. He is, however, less cautious and frugal than he used to be, borrowing from the generosity and liveliness of the Dog. Anxious and an introverted type, prudent and pessimistic—all traits of the Capricorn—are attenuated by emigration making him more dynamic, more open and confident; his second life is under the sign of sincerity, self-confidence and loyalty, all characteristics of the Dog. On one hand, life might bring difficult times upon his family, which are likely to have a deep emotional impact on him. His rewards are always his professional achievements, reaching thereby the balance he always yearned for.

The **Aquarius (Jan 20–Feb 19)**, idealist and original in everything he does, is a devoted friend, a free spirit who protects his space. Inasmuch as he is private about his own life, he is forthcoming and ready to jump in to defend a good cause. The nature of the Dog is very similar: modest, altruistic and dedicated to the good of others, which makes this year a good fit for the immigration of an Aquarius. He is inclined to believe in mysteries and unconventional theories. He may turn into a conspiracy theory fanatic, or reach a high level of spirituality. A good psychologist, he has a curious nature and is passionate for knowledge. Perhaps he's a bit too sensitive, to the point of letting his life be dominated by his thirst for knowing it all. He may become more passive, looking for ways to hide rather than showing off his qualities.

The most interesting sign in the western zodiac is **Pisces (Feb 20–Mar 20)**, especially if such a native immigrates to his new country under the influence of the Dog. Starting out drawn to mysteries, conspiracies, superstitions and esoteric passions, he gradually turns more spiritual or religious, with contradictory states of mind—swinging from exaltation to pessimism, just like a Dog. The combination of being altruistic and generous, with heavy doses of conceit and vanity, could hurt his own wellbeing. Failures could push him into depresstion in his adopted country. He will remain the ever so nostalgic emigrant, dreaming about the good old days.

YEAR OF THE
PIG/BOAR

There is a saying about people born under the sign of the **Pig**: there is no end to their good luck. The same is true for immigrants during this year: luck is on their side! Whenever they are in trouble, a helping hand saves them.

The **Pig** is honest, fond of people, optimist and a bon-vivant, treating everyone as if they are all like him. Gullible, he is easily tricked by others; however, somehow, fate will find a way to turn things around in his favor.

Everybody likes a **Pig** at the table (or on the table?!) because he is cheerful, intelligent, funny and knows how to entertain everyone. Immigration doesn't change a native fundamentally, but could touch the intimate relationship he is in, especially when his life partner has big dreams of climbing the social ladder.

He may be disheartened by either his very own family, whom he loves and is devoted to—who could manipulate his excessive tolerance—or by friends who become jealous of his endless good luck.

An **Aries (Mar 21–Apr 19)**, mostly stubborn by nature, can become indolent if given the opportunity. A generous soul, the Aries native who immigrated in the year of the Pig unselfishly dedicates himself to noble causes. He shares everything with family and friends and is very loyal to them. Although ever attracted by novelty and extravagancy, this Aries native gets bored very quickly and his enthusiasm decreases rapidly. He therefore tends to continuously change his interest of the day, minimizing his losses and being careful not to hurt people who helped him in his quests.

A **Taurus (Apr 20–May 20)** is devoted by definition, has trouble attaching himself to anyone, but when he does, it is for forever. He is rather conservative, sometimes even old-fashioned and set in his ways, and swings from being very proper to displaying a lack of manners. Unclear sometimes as to whether he has a chip on his shoulder or is just shy, immigration stimulates him. He strives to adapt and be integrated into the new world, making a point of being more native than the natives! Having a sentimental and nostalgic nature, he could also turn impulsive with bouts of rage if destiny plays games with him. Duty comes first, anywhere and anytime. Entering a new country under the influence of the sign of the Pig accentuates his sensual side; if his sexual life is disappointing, he could compensate by overeating.

American-born violinist and conductor Yehudi Menuhin is among them.

A native of **Gemini (May 21–June 20)** loves to party, trying to stick out by any means. He is the soul of a gathering, until the show is stolen by an impetuous Leo, an arrogant Sagittarius or a mysterious Scorpio. Immigration during the year of the Pig somehow provokes his destiny, accentuating his qualities, restraining his selfishness and frivolity while stressing his personal charm and charisma, confining his need for bravado, his duplicity and shallowness. All in all, he becomes even more charming, extravagant, sophisticated, thus enhancing his role of as a social butterfly.

A **Cancer (June 21–July 22)** projects the image he is in love with, living in his own world, parallel with reality, a place where there are no defects and failures, where everyone loves him, praises him and looks up to him. He doesn't break his back working, but likes to make you think he could! Well-aware on which side his bread is buttered, he pretends indifference. He knows how to find the right way and practice sentimental blackmail on people he can use and abuse. He is skillful in either using his sensitiveness to soften people, or his intelligence to win them over, all along having his sharp claws ready to punish the undeserving. The Pig cannot do much, only transfer his luck over to his adopted country where a Cancer native can live like a prince without the crown or title.

A **Leo** (**July 23–Aug 23**) enriches his destiny entering his new country under the sign of the Pig: he doubles his luck, enhances his authority, grows his wealth, has fewer fits of rage or depression, becomes more tolerant and pleasant even towards those who don't exactly rise to his level. However, he does become more snobbish and launches into glamorous adventures, being a bigger spender than he used to be; he also learns how to lose.

In his immigration, a **Virgo** (**Aug 24–Sept 22**) oscillates between salvation and victimization. He plays the role of a savior for his family, while posturing as a victim for everyone else. The female-Virgo, suspicious and analytical by nature, wants to have control in any situation. The male-Virgo is refined and elitist, elegant and a lover of beauty. Virgos have an obsession with cleanliness and health. They also can be attracted by empirical or alternative medicine. Immigration during the year of the Pig changes their luck: some re-marry, others start new beneficial relationships or change to another line of work which brings them financial satisfaction. However, in their soul, Virgos remain restless.

The **Libra (Sept 22–Oct 22)**, dynamic and enthusiastic, is an incurable optimist, a convincing orator and a talented negotiator. He thinks long and hard before throwing himself into the emigration pool, his nature being not at all adventurous or risk-taking. However, his tolerant and friendly personality could attract auspicious situations. He is dualistic and paradoxical, a skeptic with great joie-de-vivre, sensual and affectionate, a sentimental cerebral person, after all. He has a knack for bestowing balance and trust on people. To be close to a Libra is to take advantage of the proximity of wisdom itself, especially if his second life is under the sign of the Pig.

The **Scorpio (Oct 23–Nov 21)** is driven by physical pleasures, appreciates good wine, a gourmet meal, a beautiful woman, and the year of the Pig enriches it all. He is however, a difficult person, tormented by concealed desires and attracted by secrets, which, if he cannot decipher them, would only grow more mysterious. He lives on the edge of it all, and only the luck of the Pig can protect him from an overdose.

A **Sagittarius (Nov 22–Dec 21)** is usually lucky, although he sometimes simply wastes his luck. Wherever emigration may take him, he is able to create for himself a free inner space. Always avid for adventure and novelty, a tireless conqueror, he is appreciated in society by the smart ones and disliked by those below his level who also perceive him as arrogant. He's got plenty of energy and many ideas. Few of his dreams will become reality though. This Pig-Sagittarius immigrant lives beyond his means and that is stronger than his strive to reach for the top.

Romanian-born poet Paul Celan is in this group.

The most spectacular destiny change in immigration belongs to **Capricorns (Dec 22–Jan 19)** who immigrate in the year of the Pig. The unexpected success in his adopted country makes him generous, eager to do good deeds for both his native and adoptive lands alike. He dedicates himself to noble humanitarian pursuits, trying to reconcile his hands-on talent—which lays at the core of his wealth—with intense spiritual experiences.

Original, even weird, from a young age, the **Aquarius** (**Jan 20–Feb 18**) dreams to revolutionize the world. A born innovator, this immigrant in the year of the Pig believes in progress, while his humanitarian ideas, coupled with altruism and selflessness, transform him into a symbol of generosity and sacrifice for the good of his friends, his family, or the world. Even when he speaks too much and gets long-winded, one tends to listen because the Aquarius is passionate, says interesting things, has curiosity for knowledge and a good instinct for different situations which he always views from an optimistic perspective.

You never know which way a **Pisces** (**Feb 19–Mar 20**) will go. This Pig-Pisces immigrant is indecisive and elusive, he leaves you thinking he is depressed when, in fact, he is only nostalgic. He goes back and forth, would emigrate and also return home, moves forward with difficulty but is easily adaptable anywhere. He comes across as a dreamer, secluded, because of his artistic sensitivity and imagination, which can easily place him in another world. He has little understanding and empathy for the failures of people close to him, and can sail smoothly over their mishaps. Yet it is not unusual to witness moments of tenderness in him, followed by extravagant gestures, only to be forgiven for his coarseness. A roughness which is, after all, very fluid.

CARMEN FIRAN, a poet and fiction writer, has published more than twenty-five books including, novels, short stories, essays and poetry in her native Romania and in the United States. *Since 1997 she has been living in New York.* Among her recent books and publications are *Interviews and Encounters* (*Poems and Dialogue with Nina Cassian*, Sheep Meadow Press, 2016), *Inferno* (SD Press, 2014), *Rock and Dew* (Sheep Meadow Press, 2013), *Words and Flesh*, (selected works of prose, Talisman Publishers, 2008). She edited *Born in Utopia: An Anthology of Modern and Contemporary Romanian Poetry* (Talisman House, 2006), and in 2008 the anthology *Stranger at Home. Contemporary American Poetry with an Accent* (Numina Press, Los Angeles). Her work appears in translation in magazines, anthologies, and books in France, Israel, Sweden, Germany, England, Ireland, Poland. Firan is a member of the Pen American Center and the Poetry Society of America. www.carmenfiran.com

According to the Horoscope of the Immigrant, Carmen is a Ox-Sagittarius. "…Optimistic and positive, has a gift of make-believe, but solitude finds him rather melancholic. In the adopted country he bravely faces difficulties, but could be demoralized if he sees no light at the end of the tunnel…"

ALEXANDRA CARIDES, born in Romania, *emigrated to the US in 1990*. She received a PhD in Statistics from Temple University, Philadelphia, and published more than 60 articles in several journals. Currently she is Managing Editor for New Meridian Arts Press, New York, and press correspondent for the Romanian Literary Magazine *Scrisul Romanesc.* Carides published translations from English into Romanian and vice-versa, including several volumes translated from American writers: *White Fever* by Edward Foster, *Letters from America* by Deyan Brashich, *Words and Flesh* by Carmen Firan. For the last 15 years, she published translations in *The Copenhagen Review, Lettre Internationale, The Wall, Critical Flame, Raggazine, etc.*

According to the Horoscope of the Immigrant, Alexandra is a Horse-Taurus. "…loves his new home and desperately tries to adapt to it. The year of the Horse turns the Taurus into a long distance runner, who looks over his shoulder at his past without regrets…"